The House on Darkling Street

by

Annette Miller

Dedication

For my husband Brian and my sons Scot and Alex. You guys made me believe in my dreams.

Prologue

Ray Burnett tossed and turned for over an hour before he gave up and stumbled to the kitchen for a glass of water. Darkness cloaked him as he stared at the bright full moon. He could never get over how different familiar items looked at two in the morning. Ethereal light made the backyard glow, and the shadows deepened where the moon's beams didn't touch. Goosebumps broke out on his arms and he tried to rub the internal chill away. There was something different in the air, not exactly bad, but odd. What had changed tonight?

He tiptoed to the living room and pushed aside the curtains. His street looked the same as it did when he turned in. The eerie quality in the night air made him shiver again. He hurried back to his bedroom and yanked on his clothes. He stepped outside and the not-right sense intensified. He turned to stare at the large manor house sitting all alone at the end of the street. Even the moonlight avoided it.

Ray's elderly neighbor stood on her walkway and clutched her robe tight at her throat. "Ray, you felt the change in the night air, too?" She glanced at the manor before she turned to him. "I think the manor is the cause. What's going on at the Gordon house?"

"I'm not sure, Mrs. Lang." He walked over and patted her hand. "I'll go check it out. I'm sure it'll be okay."

"I've felt unrest from the Dark Lands. There could be plans we don't know about. Please be careful."

"I will. I'm sure the Dark Lands aren't responsible. At least nothing strong enough to upset the balance in Garland Falls." He shivered as a slight breeze ruffled his hair and dried the sweat on his back. "My father would have told me if there were plans to create mischief here."

He glanced up the street and his other neighbors came out. It appeared he and Mrs. Lang weren't the only ones affected tonight. People from the Dark Lands had a sixth sense about wrongness in the air. He nodded to the crowd and wondered how far the strange uneasiness spread out. He'd felt the unrest get stronger over the past week. He'd hid his nervousness from his boss so far, but he didn't know for how much longer.

Ray didn't like the eerie pull from the manor house, the darkness around it blacker than anywhere else on Darkling Street. However, he had to check it out. As the youngest resident on the street, his neighbors counted on him to take care of any problems to arise. The large, iron gates squeaked in the light breeze and tall grass waved, as if the house welcomed him in. The building sat empty for the past seven years, but now it radiated life in the pitch black of the night. An air of anticipation slammed into him, like the house waited for someone important. He swallowed hard as the manor silently beckoned him in.

His hand trembled as he pushed the gates open and stepped through. The air shouldn't be this cold, not in the middle of August. He rubbed his arms and dragged his feet up the overgrown sidewalk to the house. No night noises sounded from the woods around the sides and back of the house. As he stood in the yard, the world around him slowed to a crawl. Time itself appeared to have paused while he stared at the great house in front of him.

He took a deep breath as he stepped up to the porch and stopped. Hair raised on the back of his neck as he laid his hand on the doorknob. Boards groaned under his feet as he pushed on the unlocked door, and he stumbled back. This door had been locked for seven years. Why would it be open now? Who or what waited inside? And why did he decide to go in?

He took another deep breath before he tiptoed over the threshold. Musty air congealed in his lungs and forced him to breathe through his nose. Cold filled his chest as he stepped farther inside. He opened his mouth to call out, then thought better of it. If someone had come in, would it be smart to alert them to his presence? No, it wouldn't.

"I have to be crazy to come to this house. I shouldn't be here," he muttered. His gaze shot to the ceiling as noises from the upper floors drifted down. "I should tell the town elders what's happened and stay out of it."

He refused to let the house be one of his fears. Not much had ever scared him, and he wouldn't be scared of this place. After all, he'd lived near it for most of his adult life. He walked to the foot of the wide staircase and stopped. A loud creak echoed through the house and a light shone down the steps. The light brightened and he shielded his eyes to make out a figure in the middle of it. It figured the house would be haunted, but this ghost looked familiar.

"Henrietta?" he whispered.

"The rightful heir will arrive soon," she whispered. "You will be very important in the days ahead. You have a special purpose here, Ray Burnett. I will see you soon."

The light faded and Ray backed up and stumbled out of the house. He slammed the door behind him before he jumped down the porch steps. He yanked the iron gates closed with a loud clang that echoed through the night. Outside, he turned to stare at the manor. In a third story window, the same white light shone, then flickered out.

As soon as the light faded, the night returned to normal. Nocturnal animals went back to their hunting, crickets chirped again, and the world moved on. The air warmed and banished the strange chill to the night. Ray sprinted back to Mrs. Lang, who still stood on the walkway.

"What happened over there, Ray? What did you see?"

"Henrietta's ghost appeared." He looked at the woman, then glanced up the street. The neighbors watched as he waved to them to let them know all was well. "She said the rightful heir will arrive soon."

"Oh dear. Could she mean her brother or his daughter?"

"I don't know." He walked the older woman back to her house as the rest of his neighbors also returned to their homes. "Whoever comes, I'm pretty sure the town won't be the same."

After Mrs. Lang went inside her home, he trotted to his house, grateful to shut out the night. He locked every door and gave them a tug to be sure they wouldn't open. He turned his attention to the windows and pulled the curtains together. Even the moonlight, which he loved, gave him chills tonight. The fact Henrietta Gordon's ghost had appeared to him shook him more than he wanted to admit.

Ray went back to his bedroom and stripped down before he crawled under the covers. He shouldn't have been surprised at the unlocked door or the ghost. Strange incidents like this always happened in Garland Falls. Of course, the house on Darkling Street had never been involved before.

After seven years, the old manor had woken up. When the rightful heir arrived, would his life change? What did the arrival mean for the town? Who could this mysterious rightful heir be? He'd told his neighbor the truth. Whether it would be good or bad, Garland Falls would change in a very big way.

Chapter One

Holly Stevens drove down the main street in Garland Falls, Minnesota. "Wow, Merlin. I don't know what the celebration is, but it sure looks festive." The large cat with long, silver fur looked at her and yawned. "I know, you don't like parties, but this looks like it'll be fun." She scratched his head as he yawned again and turned around on the passenger seat.

She took the next left and turned down Darkling Street. She pulled up in front of the large manor house at the end of the dead-end street and gaped. She grabbed the photo Randolph Gordon gave her and compared the picture to the actual house. She eased out of the car and stood in the late afternoon sun. The picture didn't do the size of the place justice. The outside of the house needed to be repainted and that job might take a week by itself.

As she stared at the house, she gave silent thanks again for being able to come here. She'd never fit in with the other kids growing up, and these days, not many adults either. Daydreams filled her mind as she thought about fairies and, most of all, how great it would be to have magic. The worst was when she'd been branded a freak by the other children when she talked about magic. Her parents told her time and time again, she didn't need them and not to let their opinions bother her. So, she taught herself to stand strong.

Déjà vu slammed into her as she stood in front of the house and she leaned against her car. Garland Falls, Main Street, even the house in front of her all had a strange familiarity to them. She shook her head to make the weird sensation abate. She'd never been to Garland Falls, so why should it feel like she'd been here before? Maybe it was the magic she always thought she possessed. She turned her attention back to the manor and sighed. This wouldn't be a big job, but a huge job.

"Are you lost? Do you need some help to find someone?"

Holly whirled around and stared at the man who had spoken. His dark brown hair with reddish highlights shone in the sunlight. He towered over her, a bit on the thin side but muscular at the same time. His eyes were dark brown and filled with a kind of sadness, as if he'd seen too much bad in his life. A fierce sensation instantly gripped her. She wanted to throw her arms around him and comfort him. She shoved the urge down and cleared her throat.

"No, not a person, this house. I've been hired by Randolph Gordon to clean the place up."

She smiled when he glanced down at the magnetic door signs on her car. "I'm Holly Stevens. Sole owner, operator, and employee of Stevens House Cleaning Service." She looked at the large house in front of her, then grimaced. "I think I have to delete 'no job too big or too small.' This job is too big for one person, no matter how good my reviews say I am."

He stuck his hand out. "Raymond Burnett. I live right down the street." He paused. "You say Randolph Gordon hired you to clean up the place?"

She shook the offered hand. "Yes, he did. He wants

it ready for his daughter to take possession in thirty days, on September twenty-second. I don't know if I can get it done, but I have to."

"Oh? How come?"

She sighed. "For one thing, my reputation is at stake. A good review from Mr. Gordon will get me a lot of clients. For another, he's given me a very generous fee. I wouldn't have to worry about money for a long time. Also, he doesn't strike me as a man you want to cross."

A loud meow sounded from inside the car. Holly opened the door and picked up a large, silver-gray long-haired cat. "This is Merlin. Mr. Gordon said he could come as long as he behaves himself. Merlin, meet Raymond Burnett."

"Everyone calls me Ray." He held his hand out to the cat. "It's nice to meet you, Merlin." The cat sniffed his hand and bumped his head on Ray's palm. "I guess you want me to pet you," he said, and stroked the cat from head to tail.

"You must be special," Holly said. "He doesn't usually take to strangers. I'd better get inside and see what waits for me."

"Do you have a place to stay? Warner's B and B is nice and Miss Dee makes the best food."

She jerked her thumb toward the hulking house. "Mr. Gordon wants me to stay here to make sure no funny business goes on. He even gave me extra money for food and had the electricity and water turned on. I told him I would, but now I think I may have made a huge mistake." She turned to him and crossed her fingers. "This town does have WiFi, right?"

Ray grinned. "We got it last year. It's kind of hard

to get a signal in the middle of nowhere Minnesota, but we managed it. We needed the right people with the right skills at the right time."

"Great. I'd like to keep up with the few clients I have left back home." She grabbed her purse off the backseat. "I keep them updated on how long a job takes and when to expect me back."

Ray walked with her up to the house. "Where's your home?"

She put Merlin down and unlocked the house. "I come from a little town in the middle of nowhere Vermont, so Garland Falls is a lot like my hometown. I think I'll feel right at home here in no time."

She decided not to mention the déjà vu she'd felt when she pulled up in front of the house. She pushed the door open and dust swirled around, and she sneezed hard, echoed by her cat. The house was dark, with light coming in from the open door and the kitchen off to her right. A long hallway stretched out in front of her with a door at the end. A door she assumed to be a closet was to her left, next to the living room. More doors on the left side of the hallway were closed and there were three on the right. One was set under the staircase.

Cobwebs hung from the corners and covered the crystal chandelier above her head. She poked her head in the kitchen and groaned at the old appliances and the dirt on the floor. A green door at the back of the room, however, looked brand new. Merlin walked over to it, sniffed the crack under the door, and stared at it before he meowed at her.

"I've got my work cut out for me with this place," she said. "I hope I can get this huge job done in Mr. Gordon's timeframe."

"Tell you what," Ray said. "If you want, I can take care of the yard work while you work on the inside. You wouldn't have to worry about it and I won't even charge you. I work at Callahan's Floral Emporium so this is my job. I wouldn't do it if I didn't enjoy it."

"Sounds good." She leaned close and, in a loud whisper, said, "Mr. Gordon did say I could hire some help. He doesn't want a lot of people inside the place. He's got some serious trust issues with people in his house."

"I can understand his views. I'm not crazy about strangers in my home either." He smiled at her as he looked around. "If I stay outside, you won't have to tell Mr. Gordon I've been in the house. We wouldn't want him to get mad, right?"

When he smiled at her, her stomach did little flip flops and goosebumps covered her arms. "Right. I'd better get my car unloaded and get started. I might get at least a little bit of work done tonight. Maybe I should find a bedroom and bathroom and start there."

"Good idea. You don't want to be covered in dust before you even get to work tomorrow." He walked with her to her car and glanced inside. "Let me give you a hand with your stuff. It looks like you brought your entire home with you."

"What can I say? I have a lot of supplies. I'd better go to the store and pick up some treats for Merlin. He's been so good on this trip. He deserves a reward." After several back and forth trips up and down the long walkway, they brought up the last armload of items and set them down. "Is there a good place to eat in town?"

"Sal's Diner. They have great food and good service. You may want to get there early, though. The place fills up quick."

"Thanks for the advice. I guess we're neighbors for the next thirty days."

He smiled again, and those sweet little shivers ran up and down her back one more time. "Welcome to the neighborhood. We're glad to have you here."

After she hauled her supplies and suitcase inside, Holly waved to Ray as he walked down to his house. Time to get to work and see how much she could get done before she had to stop for dinner. If everyone in Garland Falls turned out to be as nice as him, she would have a very pleasant stay.

Chapter Two

Ray drove to Sal's Diner in the middle of Main Street after work. He got lucky and parked out front for a change. He hunched his shoulders and ducked his head to ignore the usual hostile glares he got from some of the people. He returned waves to the ones who liked him. Would Holly come here for dinner? Would she see how much people disliked him? He couldn't call himself the most popular man in Garland Falls, but he did have a few friends.

He grabbed an empty booth where he could see the door. He shouldn't look for a woman he met this afternoon. She told him the job had her here on a short time frame. When she found out he had a less than stellar reputation in Garland Falls, she might run from him like a lot of other people.

His heart leapt when she walked in and looked around. He stood and waved to her. "Would you like to join me?"

"Thanks." She raised her voice to be heard over the conversations and the clatter of silverware on dishes. "Is the diner always this full?"

He nodded and waved to a petite waitress. "Yeah. I told you they have great food and they're one of three restaurants in town."

"Only three places to eat? I guess Garland Falls is a lot smaller than my town. We have a lot of chain restaurants, fast food places, big box stores. A lot of folks were upset when the town let in the chain stores, but I guess you can't stop progress."

"You can't everywhere, but here, you can. The people like the town the way it is. Of course, when the new travel agency opened and we got more tourists, some of them have complained. Those are the ones who never come back."

The waitress came over to take their order. "Well, Ray Burnett. You haven't been in here for a long time. You haven't gone to any strange diners, have you?"

He chuckled. "Sally, you know this place is always my go to for good diner food. I wouldn't go anywhere else."

"Glad to hear it and you brought a friend with you." She turned to Holly. "Hi. I'm Sally McPhearson, proprietor, waitress, cashier, and all the other jobs it would take too long to list out. What can I get for you two tonight?"

"How about the pork chops with mashed potatoes and applesauce?" He glanced up. "Sound good to you, Holly?"

She nodded. "I love pork chops. Great choice."

"I know you want lemonade too, right?" Sally said as she scribbled on the pad she held.

Ray laughed. "It wouldn't be summer without it."

When Sally put their drinks down and scurried off, Holly opened her straw and crumpled the paper into a tiny ball. "Ray, don't take this wrong, but I noticed some people didn't look happy to see us. Is it me because I'm new here?"

He shook his head. "I hoped you wouldn't notice. No, it's me. I'm not very popular in town. A lot of people would like to see me gone. I don't socialize much and most of the folks are happy I don't."

"Sally likes you, and I know we just met, but I like you." She sipped her lemonade. "Merlin likes you, too, so you can't be all bad. Cats have a better 'people sense' than most people do." She took another sip and sighed. "This is the best lemonade I've ever had."

"I can agree on the cat sense and the lemonade."

Their food arrived and they ate in silence for several minutes. Holly sat back when she finished and put her napkin on the table. "You know, I could use some help tonight to haul some trash outside." She winked at him. "You wouldn't happen to know of someone who could lend a hand, do you?"

"I'll be happy to volunteer, Ms. Stevens. It's what good neighbors do. I'll even pay for dinner as a welcome present for you."

He smiled when her cheeks turned pink. He paid the check and they walked outside to enjoy the cool summer evening. "The general store should have some treats for Merlin. Mac should still be there." He looked at his watch. "We have time to run in to grab a few items before he closes."

They walked into the store and an older man smiled and waved. "You made it in time again, Ray. Need some last-minute supplies for the nursery?"

"Not tonight, Mac. My friend needs some cat treats and a few other supplies. We won't be long."

Holly grabbed a basket and walked up and down the aisles and bought more cat treats than were necessary. When Ray smiled at her, she shrugged. "Merlin deserves much more than I can give him. I try to spoil him all the time."

Holly followed Ray back to Darkling Street. She stopped and stared at the house, her feet frozen to the ground. "Hey, there's a light on in one of the third-floor windows." She laid a hand on his arm and he jumped a little. "Do you think someone broke in?"

"I'm not sure. This place has been abandoned for years. No one comes near it anymore."

Ray stared at the glow in the third-floor window, the same room where he'd seen the light the night before. He followed Holly up to the porch and walked in first after she unlocked the door. A loud groan from one of the upper floors reached them as Merlin streaked down the stairs and jumped into her arms. She talked to him in a quiet voice while Ray walked over to the wide staircase.

"Stay down here in case someone's up there," he said in a low voice.

She nodded and clutched Merlin tight to her chest. "I'll stay right by the door."

Ray checked every room but knew he wouldn't find anyone in the house. He'd told Holly the truth that no one had come near the house for years. Most of the town residents avoided this house like the plague. Could his imagination have gotten the better of him the other night? No. He'd seen the light and Henrietta's ghost had spoken to him.

Could Henrietta be around again? If so, he knew the light would go out by itself. Could Henrietta have made the noises, but why scare Merlin? She'd loved cats when she lived. He had a suspicion that the house and its former owner had minds of their own. He went back downstairs.

"All clear. Someone left a light on upstairs. I guess

it lit up when the power came back on." Ray frowned when she still looked shaken. "Hey, don't worry about it. This house is centuries old. The noise we heard must have been a draft that rattled a window from somewhere from the third floor."

She nodded. "You're right. I guess I'm a little spooked because I've never had to stay in the place where I clean. Those houses are all lived in and full of light and life. This place feels different. It feels neglected in more ways than one." She ran her hand down the wall. "I guess I would say it feels sad. It wants to be lived in again. It just needs a little TLC."

"You don't have to stay here." He glanced at her and watched her gaze shoot around at every little sound. "I can take you up the hill to Warner's Bed and Breakfast. Dee Warner has room and she'd be glad to have you."

She buried her face in Merlin's long fur for a moment. "I wish I could, but my contract says I have to stay here. I know Mr. Gordon wouldn't know I didn't stay, but I'd know. As soon as I get used to this place, I'll be fine. All it needs is to be cleaned up and to have some fresh air come in. Besides, this job will keep me here for only a month. Once I'm done, his daughter will move in and I'll be off to work for another client."

"If you're sure you'll be okay."

She smiled. "I'll be fine. I'll get a little more work done, then hit the sack. Wait here while I get the trash bags."

He took the bags from her and stuffed them into the trash bin by the steps. "Do you need help with anything else?" She shook her head and he petted Merlin one more time. "Then I'll let you get some rest.

My house is right down the street if you need me. I'll be over after work tomorrow to start on the yard."

"Thanks. Goodnight, Ray. I'll see you tomorrow."

Ray walked out to the sidewalk and turned. Holly still stood on the porch and he waved. She looked so small as she stood there surrounded by the huge manor. He hoped she'd be all right. After all, Henrietta still roamed her home and he knew deep down, she'd keep Holly safe if mischief lurked in the dark corners.

****

Holly locked the door and leaned against it. She'd already chosen a bedroom with a connecting bath. She'd only taken a quick look through the first floor. It looked like that floor would take the most time. The house wasn't dirty, per se—she mostly saw dust and cobwebs. Of course, it depended on how many rooms and what condition they were in. Tomorrow would be soon enough to get the scope of what else needed to be done. Merlin followed close on her heels.

"Merlin, this house is beyond creepy. I hope it feels better after we get it cleaned up. I don't think Randolph Gordon knew how big a job this would be. Come on, buddy. Let's get unpacked and try to get some sleep." She put the suitcase on the bed and flipped it open and put her clothes away. "We have a big day tomorrow and we have to keep our eye out for a large, antique brass key. Mr. Gordon says it's important and we should call him as soon as we find it."

Time to haul the vacuum up to make the room some kind of clean. She found bedding in the closet and made the bed after she vacuumed over the mattress. Small blue morning glory flowers decorated the wallpaper and the thick, quilted comforter. The whole design could be described as cute, unlike the rest of the grandiose rooms she'd passed. Merlin huffed out a breath and curled up on the foot of the bed as she threw her nightshirt next to him.

The bathroom didn't look too dirty and she had it clean in less than thirty minutes. It would still need to be scrubbed to take care of the grime ground into the grout between the tiles. She'd decided on the smallest room she'd seen so far on the second floor. The bathroom's color scheme matched the bedroom, both rooms done in blue and ivory.

Holly walked over to the window and struggled for a few minutes before she heaved it open. She inhaled the sweet summer breeze as it drifted in and filled the room with lilac, rose, and lavender. She made her number one priority in the morning to go around and open the windows. The summer scents would do a lot to banish the musty, closed up smell. The cooler Minnesota summer meant the air conditioner wouldn't be needed. Of course, all the windows needed to be scrubbed and the curtains washed.

On her initial walk-through of the house, she'd found a few doors painted different colors. Every door she tried to open was locked. The carvings on the doors were the common factor for all of them, even though the symbols were different. The green one in the kitchen had Christmas designs, and the yellow one in the hallway had a rose on it.

How many other doors would she find like those two? What was behind these doors? She'd tugged on them but they didn't open. Well, she'd look for the keys later. More important matters needed her attention first. She had to get started before her curiosity got the better of her again. She and Merlin had that in common. Neither one could stand a mystery.

She worked on a mental list of what should be tackled first. She'd already put the windows as number one. The house needed fresh air to get rid of the musty scent that clung to the furniture and other fabrics. Curtains, linens, tablecloths, towels, and any other fabrics would need to be run through the wash.

She found sheets in the bedroom closet for this room, and she expected the other bedrooms would have their linens stored in their own closets. Trash would pile up more and more once she got started with her handy implements to polish and scrub and shine.

Merlin climbed up and lay on her chest as she snuggled under the covers. "I'm glad we met Ray," she said as she ran her hand down his back. "He's way too handsome for his own good, isn't he? I had the weirdest urge to hug him when we first met him. I still want to hug him. What do you think about him?"

Merlin meowed his agreement and licked her nose. "I like him, too. I wonder why some people have a problem with him? Another question for another day." She yawned as her eyes drifted shut. "Good night, buddy. We've got a lot of work ahead of us when we get up tomorrow."

Chapter Three

The next morning, Ray walked into Callahan's Floral Emporium and found Lucas Callahan at his desk as he checked off invoices. His boss looked up when he knocked on the doorframe. "What can I do for you, Ray?"

"Wait until you hear what I have to tell you about the house on Darkling Street."

Lucas frowned a little. "You mean the big manor house on the end of your street?" He threw his pen on the desk and sat back. "What's happened?"

Ray nodded. "There's a woman there. She says she was hired to get it cleaned up by Randolph Gordon." He paused. "He wants his daughter to take possession of it."

Lucas jumped to his feet. "He doesn't have the legal right to give the house to his daughter. He knows his sister didn't want his offspring anywhere near there. I thought she had some kind of legal document drawn up to say so. I mean, I know Randolph and Henrietta parted on bad terms, but I didn't think he'd dismiss her wishes. You'd better head over to town hall and tell the elders. They'll want to know about this."

Ray frowned. "I don't even want to know what Mrs. Hall will say."

"Mrs. Hall and Henrietta Gordon could be considered friends. The rest of the town liked and respected Henrietta." Lucas cringed. "And then you have Randolph. As a member of one of the town's founding families, people were polite to him, but it didn't mean they liked him. He had more of the bad side of the Dark Lands in him. Even his sister barely tolerated him. This news will make Mrs. Hall flip and I don't even want to know how the town elders will react. I know for a fact they don't want any piece of Randolph here."

"I wish I'd known Henrietta better." Ray turned in the office doorway and grinned. "Are you sure you don't want to tell Mrs. Hall? You know she likes you best."

"Oh, no." Lucas sat back behind his desk. "This is all yours, my friend. As your boss, I delegate this particular job to you. After all, you were the first one to hear about it and Mrs. Hall likes you as much as she does me. See you soon."

Ray got in his car and headed to the town hall. He glanced at the bright banners as they waved in the summer breeze. Mrs. Hall would be in her office to work on preparations for the Founders Day party. Ever since the new travel agency opened, Garland Falls hosted more tourists than ever. Every business in town had benefitted from the influx of trade. The festivals and events had grown because of the increased traffic, and Mrs. Hall was busier than ever.

He parked in front of town hall and sat in his car for a few extra minutes and chewed his lower lip. If Randolph Gordon's daughter moved in and made significant changes, it would spell disaster for the whole town. Or would it? Henrietta's ghost did say the rightful heir would arrive soon. Did she mean

Randolph's daughter or someone else? He groaned and got out of his car. He couldn't put off telling the town elders the news any longer.

He walked into town hall and, of course, he ran into Adelaide Hall first. The stout, older lady looked to be on the way to her office. "Hi, Mrs. Hall. Have the party plans settled down yet? Can I give you a hand?"

"Oh, Ray, how nice to see you. I have some wonderful ideas and I'll need your and Lucas' help to pull off what I have in mind. I think this will be the best Founders Day celebration we've ever had."

"You know you can count on us for whatever you need." He paused and took a deep breath. "Is the mayor in yet?"

"Yes, he is. I believed he arrived a few minutes ago." She stared at him as he worried his lower lip again. "You look a bit out of sorts. What's wrong?"

"I'm not sure yet. Maybe nothing. You might want to come with me." He took her arm and led her to the short flight of stairs to the third floor. "I think you'll want to hear this."

Ray and Mrs. Hall entered the mayor's office as the man himself and the town elders settled in for their work day. "Mayor Jacobs, do you have a few minutes?" Ray said. The mayor scowled at him and he backed up a couple of steps. "I promise I won't take up too much of your time."

The mayor sat behind his desk and frowned. When Mrs. Hall glared at him, he cleared his throat and sat back. "Mr. Burnett, you always bring me more problems than I expect. Whatever you have to say must be important for Adelaide to come with you." He folded his hands and sighed. "Let's hear your news."

Ray stared at the elders. The next words out of his mouth would upset everyone in the room. "Randolph Gordon's daughter is moving into the house on Darkling Street. She should arrive within the next thirty days."

As expected, loud voices echoed through the mayor's office, as each member shouted to make himself or herself heard over everyone else. The mayor jumped to his feet and banged his fist on his desk several times until he had everyone's attention.

"How do you know this, Ray?" Mayor Jacobs narrowed his eyes as he leaned forward. "Has Randolph been in touch with you? I wouldn't be surprised if he called you. You Dark Landers have a tendency to stick together."

"No, sir. I've never spoken to Randolph Gordon." He glanced at Mrs. Hall and she gave him a small nod. "I met the woman he hired to clean up the place. She's the one who told me about his plans."

Mayor Jacobs jumped to his feet and leaned on his desk. "And who is this woman? Is she part of Gordon's plan?"

"I don't believe so. She said she's there for thirty days to get the place ready before Randolph's daughter arrives. Her name is Holly Stevens. From the decals on her car, she owns a house cleaning service."

"Well, this news has started our day off in a bad way. We don't know what kind of mischief the Gordon girl will bring with her. Randolph must not have the Master Key or he would have moved in himself, instead of his daughter. Keep an eye on this Holly Stevens and let us know as soon as you hear any other news you think is important."

"Yes, sir."

"Come along, Ray," Mrs. Hall said. She led him out of the mayor's office, down to her office, and shut the door. "Don't let them get to you. Those blustering old fools will sit around and shout more than talk about a plan. They won't stop until they make themselves hoarse. I know. I've dealt with Theodore and his cronies for far too many years. Sit down. You and I need to discuss this calmly."

"Mrs. Hall, what should I do? I live on the same street and I offered to help Holly with the yard work. There's a lot of yard around the Gordon house to maintain." He glanced at her. "Lucas said you would flip at this news."

She winked at him "Well, Mr. Lucas Callahan doesn't know me as well as he thinks he does." She patted Ray's hand before she squeezed it. "There's not a lot you can do right now and we don't know how Randolph's daughter will act when she arrives. She might have grown out of her nasty attitude, but knowing Randolph, I don't think so. She took after him more than her aunt." Mrs. Hall sat back with a twinkle in her eyes. "Tell me about this Holly Stevens. What is your impression of her?"

Ray thought for a few minutes. "I feel she's a good person. She has a cat, and you know cats don't stay around people they don't like. She's shorter than me with long black hair and green eyes and she's a little on the thin side. She's down to earth and she's got a great smile. I bet she's a lot stronger than she looks."

Mrs. Hall laid a finger on her lips and smiled. "You have an eye for detail about this woman. I don't think you've ever described anyone else in such a complete manner. Do you mean she has physical or emotional strength?"

He shrugged as his cheeks heated. "Maybe both?" he said, not sure which quality he should give more importance to. "There's something about her I can't quite put my finger on. I think she's got magic but I don't know what kind it is. She's got a different quality, a different feel than the people here. Could she be the one the house waited for these last seven years? Henrietta did say one day someone would come who would take her place."

"We all thought she meant Randolph, the stuffy old goat, or one of his children." Mrs. Hall straightened a stack of papers on her desk. "Maybe you should get to know Holly better. The Gordon house is huge and I'm sure she'd appreciate any help you can give her." She smiled. "Take her some cookies from Heavenly Bites or maybe some of Dee Warner's cinnamon rolls. Delicious treats are always a nice welcome gift to the neighborhood."

"True." Ray nodded. "You've given me a great idea. I'll take her some when I go on my lunch break." He checked the time on his phone and stood. "Speaking of which, I've got to get back to work. Do you think I should take her some lunch?"

"What a wonderful idea. Go for it, dear boy."

Ray smiled as he drove back to the nursery. Lunch with Holly Stevens was a wonderful idea indeed. How nice would it be if she were the rightful heir to the house on Darkling Street? It would sure be nice for him.

Chapter Four

Holly coughed and sneezed as she took down the curtains and opened the windows. She stared at the sunlight as it shone on the mocha-colored leather couch and sighed. "This couch matches the uncomfortable chair in Mr. Gordon's office. Doesn't this family believe in any other fabric besides leather? What's your opinion of this awful furniture, Merlin?"

The cat sniffed the couch a few times and walked away, his tail in the air. Holly laughed and scooped him up. "I had those exact same thoughts. I'll have to go into town and get some lunch soon. The kitchen is almost done, but I can't put any food in the fridge until I get it replaced. I don't think there's enough cleanser on the planet to make it smell better."

She gave her cat one last squeeze before she put him down and looked around the room. In a back corner stood a narrow, blue door with a snowflake and what looked like a small fairy carved into it. She walked over to it and reached out to turn the ornate, silver knob. She snatched her hand back as the cold metal burned her fingers.

"Why is this door so cold? I've heard of metal so cold it burns the skin, but this is a whole new level of cold," she murmured. "Could it be a type of refrigerated storeroom?"

She went to the kitchen and returned with an oven

mitt. She tried to turn the doorknob one more time and found it locked. "Interesting. This is the third door with designs carved into it. The green one in the kitchen has Christmas images on it. The yellow one in the hall by the front door has a rose, and now this blue one with a snowflake. I wonder how many doors we'll find like this?"

She trotted to the hall door and tugged on it, not surprised to find it locked as well. "I bet the one in the kitchen is locked, too. What do you think, Merlin? Should we try it?"

She walked to the door in the kitchen and turned the knob with the same result. However, faint music drifted to her from behind it. She laid her ear against the wood and frowned at Merlin, who sat quietly at her feet. "Christmas music? It's the middle of August. What the heck is going on here?"

Someone knocked at the front door and she jumped. Her heart accelerated to beat about a thousand times a minute and her breath came out in shallow gasps. Nothing like a surprise guest to get the adrenaline pumping. Who could possibly be there? No one in Garland Falls knew she was here. Her eyes lit up and she smiled. No one knew but a certain Ray Burnett.

She tossed the oven mitt on the kitchen table and dusted off her hands on her jeans. She opened the door and Ray stood there. Her stomach flip flopped and did a happy dance. He held two paper bags, a small one and a larger one with suspicious grease spots. He held a cardboard drink carrier with two cups in his other hand.

"Hi," she said, her heart now beating faster for a whole different reason. "I didn't expect to see you again so soon. Did you want to come in?"

He stared at the interior of the house and smiled. "Thanks, but it's a nice day and I like to be outside. It's a little after twelve, and I thought you might be hungry." He held up the bag. "I brought you lunch."

She pointed to the two cups. "And lunch for you as well, or am I wrong?"

He grinned. "Guilty as charged. It's my lunch hour. Would it be all right if we ate together?"

"Of course." She walked over to the small table with two chairs on the porch and swept off the leaves. "Sorry the chairs are a little dirty. I haven't been out here to clean up yet. I finished the kitchen not too long ago. The living room is huge and will probably take most of this week. I've already started a list of what to tackle first. I might as well start at the bottom and work my way up."

He glanced at the dirt on his pants and the dust and grime on hers. "Then I'd say it's time for a break, and I don't think a little more dirt will hurt either one of us."

She laughed. "Very true." She looked at the peeling paint on the porch and the walls. "The place needs a fresh coat of paint and a whole lot more work than I thought when I first saw it."

"You're right. It's going to be a very big job." Ray divided up the food from the first bag and laid the food on napkins. "I got you a cheeseburger. I hope it's okay."

"With fries?"

"Of course. What's a burger without fries?" He put one of the cups in front of her. "I got us each a lemonade since you liked it so much at dinner the other night. Sal's has the best lemonade around."

She took a sip and closed her eyes. "You're right.

It's so fresh and not too tart or too sweet. It's much better than what you'd get in any store."

"Sally makes it herself from scratch every day in the summer. She says summer is when it tastes the best." He ate a few fries. "There's also not much call for it in the winter."

Holly finished her burger, then wiped her hands on an extra napkin. "Sal's Diner has the most delicious food I've ever eaten. I may stay here forever to eat."

If she stayed in Garland Falls, he would be very happy. Ray put the other bag on the table and reached inside. "I also brought dessert. There's a cookie shop in town called Heavenly Bites. I thought you might like something sweet to finish up on."

Her cheeks warmed as she stared at him and she dropped her gaze. The cookies weren't the only sweet thing on this porch. He'd gone on his lunch break and thought of her. How much sweeter could he get?

He pulled out four cookies. Two were chocolate chip and two were sugar cookies covered in rainbow sprinkles. He laid one of each on a napkin and slid it over in front of Holly. She picked up the chocolate chip and took a bite. She chewed and closed her eyes as she savored the sweetness of the cookie.

"This is the best cookie I've ever had," she said. "How do they make it taste so good? It's sweet, but not so sweet that I can't taste every ingredient."

Ray looked down before he glanced up with a small smile. "It's all done with magic."

****

After Ray had gone, Holly went inside and sat on the couch. Merlin jumped up next to her and laid his paw on her thigh. She stroked him as her mind

29

wandered to Ray again. "You know what, buddy? Ray Burnett is such a handsome guy. I know you don't notice things like this, but I sure did. His hair is brown, but in the sun, it has deep red highlights."

Merlin meowed and crawled onto her lap. She leaned back and he lay on her chest, his head so close to her face, his whiskers tickled her cheek. "He's also got dark brown eyes and boy, is he built." Merlin meowed again and she giggled as she scratched his ears. "No, silly, not like some super buff guy. He does work at a nursery, so moving all those heavy plants has given him some pretty nice arms."

She stared off into space and thought about him. "It's more than his looks, Merlin. He always looks sad or afraid of people. Here's another weird point to make. As soon as I saw him, I knew he'd be important to me." The cat meowed and she shook his paw. "Yes, I meant to us. I wonder if there's any truth to love at first sight or does it only happen in fairy tales? I could swear it happened to me when he introduced himself to us."

Merlin batted her nose and she nuzzled him. "I know we have to get back to work, but I'd like to take a few minutes to daydream." When he batted her nose again, she sighed and stood, putting him on the floor. "Fine. We'll get some more work done before we quit for dinner. I think I need to make Sal's Diner one of our regular stops. We could both eat very well there."

A strong breeze that blew in through the open windows disturbed more dust and she sneezed again. A large roll-top desk stood next to the narrow blue door at the back of the room. She pushed up the cover and it moved about an inch. Holly took a deep breath, worked her fingers into the gap, and gave a huge shove upward.

It flew open and a large, antique brass keyring hit the wood floor with a loud clang. There were at least thirteen keys on it. Three had designs similar to the doors she'd discovered.

Merlin sniffed at it and looked up at Holly. She picked it up, and stared at it as she turned it over in her hand. The keys warmed her palm as she stared at all of them. Dust covered the desktop, the dark brown turned a paler shade, but the keys looked brand new. They'd been locked away for years, so how could they be warm? She curled her fingers around the ring as it vibrated in her grasp. She stared at the cat, who cocked his head at her.

"What do you think, buddy? Could these keys open those locked doors we found?" She shrugged. "One way to find out."

She walked back out to the yellow door in the hall and found the key with a rose carved into it. As the key slid easily into the lock, she closed her eyes and took a deep breath. She turned the key, with no result. She stared at the key, and it had the same rose as the door. Weird it didn't work.

"Well, I didn't expect complete disappointment and an anti-climactic end. Let's try the other doors." She glanced down at Merlin, who stared at her like he didn't know what she waited for. "I should tell Mr. Gordon about this. After all, if I can't get into these locked rooms, I can't clean them."

Holly matched the other keys to their doors with the same result. If there were thirteen keys, there should be thirteen doors, but she'd only found three so far. She returned the keyring to the desk and decided to forget about them and their doors for now. Unless Mr. Gordon wanted her to get in there to clean up. She'd talk to her temporary employer and ask what he wanted her to do.

With her mind made up, she grabbed her bucket with all the supplies in it and got to work. She rubbed all the woodwork with a special beeswax blend she'd created until the original luster shone in the afternoon light. She grabbed her vacuum from where she left it in the upstairs bedroom. She bought the best vacuum on the market, but even it couldn't get all the dirt out of the rug.

"Okay," she said to Merlin, who had perched on the couch to watch. "This rug is beautiful, but I think I need a better machine to get all the dirt out. I might be able to save it." She ran her fingers over the fibers. "It'd be a shame to have to replace it. It complements the room really well. I wonder if one of the stores on Main Street has a steam vac? Those machines can get dirt out of any kind of rug."

She turned to the fireplace and rolled her eyes. With all the old ash and who knew what else resided in there, she would have to use her shop-vac to get all the grunge out. She opened a plastic tarp and laid it over the floor, to cover as much of the area rug as she could. If more dirt got into it, her job would be harder and take longer. Merlin watched her drag in the large, round machine, then bolted from the room.

"I know," she called. "You don't mind the vacuum, but you don't like this machine because it makes way too much noise." She chuckled as she set up the shop-vac. "Scaredy cat."

Chapter Five

Holly grabbed a facemask out of her bag and settled it over her nose and mouth. She had no desire to breathe in whatever lurked in there. She grunted as she removed old half-burned logs and a huge pile of ash. The metal grate had rusted in several spots and she set it on the porch. It would need to be sanded and re-painted. After she finished, she got on her knees to scrub the interior. A loud groan escaped her as it took longer than expected to get all the burn marks to fade.

A tap on her leg made her stick her head out. She grinned at her cat as he stared at her. "I'm almost done with the fireplace, Merlin. The living room itself will take at least another day, maybe more, to finish. It's the largest room on this floor. I'll have to call Mr. Gordon to see what he wants me to do about the chimney. I'm sure it needs to be cleaned out and maybe some repair work." She paused for a minute. "Do you think Ray will come by again?" She laughed when Merlin meowed. "I hope so, too."

The whole time she worked, she couldn't get Ray Burnett out of her mind. He had beautiful eyes and treated her with the utmost respect. She hoped she'd get to see him again, maybe even go on a real date. She finished the inside of the fireplace and crawled out to stretch her back. She ignored the dirt covering her from head to toe. Soot and grime covered the bricks in layers thicker than what coated her. It would take a whole day to clean those. A loud knock echoed through the house.

She walked to the front door as Merlin trotted along behind her. "We have company again, buddy, and I'm a complete mess." She opened the door as Ray lifted his hand, ready to knock one more time. Her heart fluttered in her chest as she gazed at him. "Hi. Sorry it took me a minute to get here."

"I didn't know where you'd be in the house," he said. "I didn't know if you heard me. You look like you've been hard at work."

She stepped aside and let him come in. "I have. I worked on the kitchen this morning. I'm glad there weren't a lot of dishes to wash. The floor is in good shape and the cabinets weren't hard to clean. The refrigerator will have to go and the rest of the appliances as well. They're out of date and haven't been used in a long time. I started the living room after lunch, and it's a bigger job than I anticipated."

Ray peeked into the room and whistled. "You aren't kidding. I know I said I'd take care of the outside, but can I help you in here, too?"

"Do you think you could clean the chandelier? Even with my ladder, I'm not tall enough to reach the top of it." She glanced over her shoulder. "If Mr. Gordon had any idea how big a job this would be, he would've let me hire an army. I know he doesn't want a lot of people in here, but wow. The man has some serious trust issues."

He crossed his arms. "Like I said earlier, the Gordons were very private people. If he didn't want anyone in here, you should've made me stay on the porch."

She laughed. "I probably should have, but I refuse to be rude. Besides, I've accepted your offer of help with the yard and we've had two meals together. I don't think you count as a stranger anymore. I need help with the chandeliers and some of the other high places. What brings you by, besides yard work?"

"It's right around dinner time and I thought I'd take you to the diner again. I finished work and wanted to eat before I started out here."

She raised an eyebrow, and her smile grew wider. "I see. Well, you are mighty good neighbor, Mr. Burnett. I accept." She looked at her hands, arms, and clothes. "I can't go like this. Could you wait for a few minutes while I get cleaned up and change? I'm a real mess."

Ray glanced around the house. "I don't mind at all. I'll stay in the living room and not poke around. Think Mr. Gordon would be okay if I sit and not move?"

"I'm sure he would. I'll just be a few minutes." Merlin stalked over to Ray and jumped into his lap when he sat on the couch. "At least you'll have some company."

Holly rushed through a quick shower and grabbed clean clothes from the large wardrobe she appropriated. She gave her shirt a vigorous shake, to snap out some of the wrinkles. Thank goodness her jeans looked all right. She pulled out her flats, and hopped on one foot first, then the other as she put them on. No time for makeup, but he did see her covered in dust and dirt, so even no makeup would be a vast improvement.

"I'm ready," she said as she walked down the wide staircase.

Ray held onto Merlin as he stood. "You look

great."

Her face warmed and she ducked her head. "Thanks. Let me lock up and we can go."

Soon, they were in his car headed for the small diner. Main Street was busy and Ray had to park a few blocks away. They hurried to the diner and waited for several minutes until a booth opened up. As soon as they sat down, a tall man with tawny hair, a black cowboy hat set a jaunty angle on his head came over.

"Hi, Ray. Who's your friend?"

"Lucas, this is Holly Stevens. Randolph Gordon hired her to clean his sister's house so his daughter can move in." He turned to Holly. "This is Lucas Callahan, my boss."

She shook Lucas' hand. "It's nice to meet you. Ray says you own a florist shop and nursery. I'll be down to see you some time in the future. The grounds around the house need a lot of work. I'd also like to add some bouquets around the inside to make the house feel more like a home."

"I look forward to your visit at the floral emporium." He clapped Ray on the shoulder. "Ray's great at yardwork and has a good eye for what would bring out the best in a garden. I can give him some extra time off if you find you need him more often. We've already got most of the orders ready for the Founders Day party. I might even be able to cut you a deal on what you need."

"Thank you, Lucas. I appreciate your generous offer. I can promise I'll bring some business to you."

"And it will be much appreciated. I'll let you two get back to your dinner. My wife got back from out of town today and I'm here to pick up dinner for us." He winked at them. "I'm in a bit of trouble for the way I let the house go while she was gone on her assignment. It wouldn't be bad if I wasn't such a slob."

"My job is to clean houses and I'm pretty good at it," Holly said. "If you need any help, let me know. I'll be glad to lend assistance."

Lucas chuckled. "And your offer will get you a big discount at my shop."

They watched as Lucas walked back to the counter and leave with two plastic bags. Holly turned back to Ray. "He's very nice."

"Lucas is great to work for. I'm lucky he hired me."

She frowned a little. "Why? You don't act like a troublemaker." She leaned forward to whisper, "You don't have a criminal past, do you?"

He shook his head. "No, no criminal history. My…father…and his side of the family don't have the best reputation in Garland Falls. The people here like my mom okay, but they aren't thrilled with my dad."

The waitress, Sally, set two glasses of water down and hurried off with a quick promise to be right back.

Holly opened the menu and stared at the contents for a moment. "So, you're guilty by association."

He looked down at the menu and picked at the corner. "You hit the nail on the head."

She crossed her arms on the table. "What an unfair attitude. I've known you for one day and I can tell you're a good guy."

"I appreciate your generous opinion, but we've spent very little time together."

Sally returned, order pad in hand. "Ray Burnett, this is the most I've seen you in here in a long time."

He chuckled. "Sally, you know I get here when I can. I've been busy and you know how a lot of the folks in this town feel about me. I'm not very popular. You remember Holly?"

"Of course, I do. Nice to see you again, Holly. Ray, people here don't know you like a lot of us do. After all, Mrs. Hall has given you her stamp of approval and so has Dee Warner. Their opinions should be good enough for anyone. Now, what'll you two have?"

"I can't decide," Holly said. "It all sounds so good."

Ray handed their menus to Sally. "How about the meatloaf with scalloped potatoes and green beans. Let's have lemonade, too."

"You got it, Ray. You always know when we have meatloaf on the menu." She winked. "Even before I have a chance to list it on the Specials Page."

She hurried away and Holly watched her give their order to the cook before she rang up several customers. "Doesn't anyone else work here? It looks like she does every job but cook."

"She's a wonder, all right. I guess she'd hire more help if she didn't love the hectic pace." Ray gazed at Holly. "So far, so good with the house and all?"

"Yep. Of course, I've gotten the bedroom and the bathroom I moved into finished. The living room is taking more time than I thought it would. The kitchen is done except for getting new appliances. Tomorrow, I'm down to twenty-eight days." She rested her head on her hand. "Mr. Gordon has given me an impossible deadline. This house is huge. If he wanted it done by a certain date, why didn't he hire someone sooner?"

"I don't have an easy answer for you." Ray sipped

his water. "I can start the yardwork tonight. I might not get a lot done, but I can at least make a list of what I need to do. Since I live right up the street, I can work until it gets too dark to see."

She reached across the table and squeezed his hand. "Thanks." She leaned back as Sally brought their dinners over. "He gave me extra money to hire whomever I needed. I guess I hired you and I want to pay you for your help. Especially if you leave work early to come work with me."

"I knew you had a generous heart." They finished dinner and paid the bill, then walked outside. "Have you had a chance to see the rest of Main Street yet?"

Holly turned her face into the soft, summer breeze as it carried the fragrant aroma of different flowers to her. "Just what we saw the other night when you were kind enough to buy me dinner. I've been super busy at the house. It's too nice a night to go right home and the sun hasn't even set yet."

As they walked down the street, Holly laced her fingers through his and moved a little closer to him, all without a second thought.

Chapter Six

"A few stores down from the diner is Heavenly Bites," Ray said as he pointed to it. "You already went to the general store. At the end of Main Street are the town hall and the library. The other restaurants are on Grape Street along with some more stores."

"Has Garland Falls grown much?" Holly glanced around Main Street. "It doesn't look big enough to support all these stores."

"It hasn't grown by leaps and bounds, but a couple of new businesses did open up." He pointed across the street. "The leather shop is new and the lady who runs it is married to my boss' brother. A new travel agency opened at the start of last year."

She nodded as she checked out the leather store and the others on both sides of the street. "This street looks like the place to open up a new shop. With the loss of some of my clients back in Vermont, this town might be the place for me. Maybe I could add my own business here."

Ray fought to keep his excitement down at her words. If Holly stayed, he'd have one more ally against the prejudice that constantly dogged him. "Garland Falls likes new people and new businesses. It keeps the town fresh."

She cocked her head. "Garland Falls likes new people or do the residents like new people?"

"Maybe both. After all, the town is its own self."

She nudged his shoulder. "I find your perspective very interesting, Ray. Not many people speak of their town as if it's alive."

"Not many people know how special Garland Falls is. I think the town likes you, though." He smiled at her look. "Mac never stocked so many cat treats until you came here. It's a good sign."

Warmth from her small hand bled into his as her callouses pressed into his palm. They matched with his own from all the hard work he did at the nursery. He didn't want to talk about the town any longer. He wanted to know if she had been serious when she said she might move here. He wanted to ask about her and why she held his hand. He also wanted to know why she had such a special hold over him. Of course, he couldn't complain about it, though.

"The park behind town hall is where most of our events take place." He hesitated, then said, "I'm surprised Randolph Gordon hired someone from outside Garland Falls."

"Caught me off guard, too. He found out I lost several clients this year. Some of them were elderly and the families decided they didn't need my service any longer. So, I lost almost half my income when they moved in with their kids." She walked a little closer to him. "Randolph said he researched my company and liked what he found."

He squeezed her hand. "I'm sorry to hear you lost some business, but I'm glad you came here. Are the lost clients the main reason you took this job?"

"Yeah. I had too much time on my hands and had put feelers out to pick up more clients," she said. "I also needed the money and Mr. Gordon offered an amount I couldn't say no to. I mean like a major amount of dollar signs."

Ray nodded. He could understand what she meant. Money made the world go around. "I guess I should get you back. Would you like to meet Dee Warner? She runs Warner's Bed and Breakfast and she makes the best cinnamon rolls."

She sighed, as a dreamy smile curved her lips. "You had me at cinnamon rolls. Sure, tell me when so I can look better than I do when we decide to get dinner or lunch." She grinned at him, not able to resist a small tease. "I think the best time to catch me when I'm clean is at breakfast time. I want to get up early to get a jump on the work. At least the living room is almost done."

"I'll come get you for lunch around noon." He held up their clasped hands. "Will you hold my hand again? If so, I hope you realize I wouldn't be opposed to it."

She jerked her hand away. "I'm so sorry. I don't want you to think I'm always this forward. It felt right." He smiled as her cheeks turned pink. "And I'd love to have lunch with you again. Thank you, Ray."

They walked back to his car and he drove her back to Darkling Street and the silent house waiting for them.

****

After Ray dropped her off, Holly sagged against the door when she went inside. She'd held his hand? She'd never held anyone's hand on the spur of the moment before in her life. She just met the man, for pity's sake. Her common sense took a hike as soon as they were close enough to touch. Merlin meowed at her feet.

"Don't judge me, buddy. I didn't stay out too late."

She pushed off the door and went to the kitchen. She handed Merlin a few cat treats before she opened his food. "You are one spoiled cat."

She placed his bowl on the floor and walked out to the large staircase. She knew the long, twisted banister would take one day by itself to do. "I have to get this done," she murmured. "If not, I don't get all the money he promised and he'll give me a bad review."

She walked back to the roll-top desk in the living room. She picked up the brass keyring and stared at it. Her hand warmed it and it vibrated a little again. "Why the heck do these keys vibrate every time I pick them up?" She bounced them once in her hand. "More important, why do I let it bother me?"

She walked out and turned down the hallway. A dark purple door with an onyx knob set into the wall under the stairs gave her the creeps. One key jumped in her hand. The carvings on this door were of a darker nature, with what could only be described as monsters. She looked toward the front door, and wished she'd turned on the hallway light instead of just the foyer light. The key jerked again and pulled her toward the door.

"I can take a hint," she muttered. "Don't be so pushy."

The key almost dragged her hand toward the door. She inserted the key and turned it. The lock clicked but didn't open. She frowned and tried again with the same result. "I guess you don't want to open either."

She tugged on the key and it wouldn't come out of the lock. "Come on, you stupid door. Give me back the key." Her muscles strained as she pulled with both hands. "I don't know who's decided to hold onto this key, but let go."

She braced one foot against the door and her muscles strained as she pulled on the key. "It's impossible for a door to hold onto a key." One more hard yank, and the key flew out and she stumbled back against the opposite wall. The door bowed, like some force hit it from the other side. "I'm not sure what just happened, but I don't like it and I hope it doesn't happen again."

Merlin stood in front of her, his back arched, his fur straight up, and he hissed at the door. When she moved, he moved to keep himself between her and the door. The key settled down and hung with the rest like the weirdness never happened. Holly held the keyring up and stared at it.

"Don't worry, buddy. I will never, ever in a million years open the creepy door under the stairs." She backed away toward the front of the house. "I think we've done enough for one day. Maybe we should go upstairs to bed."

She made sure to turn on the upstairs hall light before she climbed the steps. She went down to her small, comfortable room, and let out a sigh of relief when she locked the door behind her and Merlin. There were at least six rooms on this floor and who knew how many on the third floor.

She felt sure the house had an attic and it would be huge. With her luck, it would be crammed with junk. Maybe she'd let Randolph's daughter deal with the attic situation. Again, she'd worry about it when the time came, if it ever did. She would have to make serious progress tomorrow if she expected to finish on time.

She snuggled under the covers as Ray crept into

her thoughts and pushed the strange purple door out of her mind. Why did she find herself so drawn to him and in such a short amount of time? Sure, he had good looks, okay, great looks, and she'd always been a sucker for tall guys.

But she'd fallen for him almost as soon as she saw him. She hadn't known him for a full day before she'd decided she liked him. She'd had such a good time with him at dinner and then when they walked around the town. Garland Falls looked like a picture-perfect place to live, and Ray made it better. His hand warmed hers when she held it. Strange how their callouses matched up perfectly.

The dark purple door intruded on her thoughts again, and with heavy reluctance, she let it snatch her attention away from Ray. Some kind of person or monster lived on the other side. She'd be happy to never find out who or what lurked back there. The door in the living room almost gave her frostbite after one second of contact. The door in the kitchen had Christmas music behind it. Who knew what the one in the hall hid. Who the heck lived behind all those doors, and would she find more on the other floors? More importantly, would she want to?

"Merlin, I have way too many questions. I think we'll leave all those doors alone." The cat walked up the bedspread and curled under her arm and purred in her ear. "Thanks, buddy. I knew you could help me. You're the absolute best."

She held him tight, closed her eyes, and hoped sleep would overtake her in a matter of minutes.

****

Ray sat in his kitchen and drank a glass of water.

He couldn't get Holly Stevens out of his mind. He'd never met anyone so fun and smart. She had to be the most beautiful woman he'd ever seen. He'd been right about what he'd said to Mrs. Hall. Holly had emotional strength and physical strength. He knew she could handle whatever the manor could throw at her. If he could rid himself of the unease crawling up his spine every time she walked inside, he'd feel a lot better.

The Gordon house had always had an odd quality to it, more so after Henrietta Gordon passed away. The atmosphere around it changed and he felt the house almost dared anyone to enter. He could count on one hand the number of people in Garland Falls who'd been inside the place. Most avoided it like the plague. He sat back and failed to banish the dark thoughts from his mind. Most of the people in Garland Falls avoided him the same way.

The town had expected Henrietta's brother, Randolph, would come back for the funeral. Of course, the siblings had been estranged for years before he had moved away. Even so, their family solicitor would have contacted him and asked him to come back to take care of the estate. But he'd never shown or called the town elders to say what he wanted to do with the place.

Randolph had let the house stand empty for seven long years. The taxes were paid annually, but maintenance and upkeep hadn't been considered. Then out of the blue, Holly showed up. Could it be a coincidence she'd been chosen to come here? Everyone in Garland Falls knew you had to have magic in you to find the town unless it wanted to be found. The town had no problem with the tourist trade, because it had become a popular vacation spot.

Holly had a special quality, but what could it be and why? Ray put his glass in the sink and went up to bed, as the question still burned in his mind. She'd held his hand tonight and said it felt right. It felt right to him, too. His mother often told him every being in the fairy realm had a perfect match. Could Holly be his? Or did he wish it so he could make peace with his Dark Land side.

He did his nighttime routine and sat on the edge of the bed. The gold door in his room opened and a tall woman stepped through. Her light brown hair had daisies woven through it and matched the floor-length, pale-yellow dress she wore. A gold belt circled her waist, a perfect mate to the ring on her left hand.

He jumped to his feet and hugged her. "Mom, what are you doing here? Is there a problem in Nature's realm? If so, you know I can't go there to help you."

"All is well there." She kissed his cheek. "I sensed your conflict. What troubles you?"

He walked back to his bed and sat. "I'm not in conflict. I mean, I don't think I am. I met a girl who was hired to work on the Gordon house. She's special and I can't figure out why."

His mother sat beside him. "If she stayed in the house after a full day, then she is special indeed. Why is she here?"

"Randolph Gordon hired her to clean it up." He stared at his mother. "He wants his daughter to move in."

"I thought Henrietta didn't want him or his family to move into her home." She tapped her chin. "Why would he disregard her wishes so blatantly?"

"Who knows?" He glanced at his mother, then

shrugged. "He wants Holly to have it done in thirty days."

"He wants her to clean his sister's massive house in thirty days? I wonder what his reason could be." His mother began to pace. "Do the town elders know?"

He nodded. "I told them when I found out why she came. They want me to keep them updated, and I know I have to, but it feels like a betrayal. I've gotten to know Holly a little and I know she's not here to cause any problems."

His mother placed her finger under his chin and raised his face. "I believe, even after such a short time with this woman, you've already lost your heart to her." She kissed his forehead. "Don't let her hurt you, my dear. I love you too much to see you in any more pain."

"I won't. After all, she's here for a month. I doubt a serious relationship will develop between us."

She chuckled as she smoothed his hair back. "I know love when I see it. You have begun to fall for this Holly. I pray it's not a mistake. Sleep well, my darling."

After his mother returned to Light Side lands, Ray thought about her words. He'd fallen for Holly the moment she took his hand. Did she have the same feelings for him? He got under the covers and settled down for the night. He would find out more tomorrow, but he hoped she liked him as much as he had started to like her.

Chapter Seven

Every creak, every groan that echoed through the house had Holly lying on one side, then flopping to the other. With all the work she'd done, she'd expected to be asleep in minutes, but nope. It must be almost dawn by now. She stared at the clock and fell back. She'd been in bed for about an hour and it felt like the longest hour ever.

She punched the pillow and turned over again. Merlin sat up and let out a low growl as he stalked to the end of the bed, and she shot straight up. White light shone under the door and she watched as a shadow blocked it out for a second, like someone walked in front of it. Why didn't she get Ray's phone number before he left earlier? She could use some company right about now and he'd be great backup for whoever had gotten in.

She threw the covers back and tiptoed to the door to listen. The light went out and the footsteps retreated. Merlin stood next to her and looked up. "Should we check it out?" she whispered. "If nothing else, we can bolt for the front door and get Ray."

Merlin meowed and put his nose to the space where the door didn't quite reach the floor. Holly took a deep breath and eased the door open a crack. She didn't see the light or hear any other noises.

She stepped into the hallway and looked left and

right. "This has got to be the worst of very bad ideas," she mumbled.

Merlin walked in front of her and stopped at the stairs leading to the third floor. She stood next to him and walked behind him when he started up. Her hands shook as she climbed the stairs, but from fear or the cool night air, she couldn't decide.

"This has got to be the craziest idea I've ever had, including the time I tried the zipline adventure weekend." As she reached the landing, she saw the light disappear behind a door at the end of the hallway. "Do I need to do this?" She hesitated and took a deep breath before she continued forward. "I may as well. I've come this far. If I don't, I'll wonder what's behind there and it will keep me up for the rest of the night."

She laid her hand on the ornate doorknob and turned it. The door swung open, to reveal a bedroom with floor to ceiling windows that looked out over the back garden, the drapes tied to either side. Holly stepped in and marveled at the size of the canopy bed. A white scroll frame with butterflies in the pattern on the headboard complemented the pale-yellow bedspread. The crocheted, ivory canopy had little yellow roses interspersed at the cross sections.

Matching white furniture sat at comfortable places around the room. A marble fireplace took up most of one wall, with tall windows on either side, looking over the front lawn. A plush chair and small table were off to her right. Pictures in silver frames sat from one end of the mantel to the other. A vase on the table held roses long dead.

She walked over and picked up the middle picture. A man and woman stood not too close together, he with a slight frown, her with a genuine smile. Holly recognized the man as Randolph Gordon, so the woman must be his sister. Henrietta Gordon looked like a pleasant woman someone people could go to with their problems.

"I wish I could have met you, Ms. Gordon," she murmured. "You look easier to get along with than your brother, and a lot nicer, too."

"Many people said so when I lived here."

Holly dropped the picture and swung around. The ghost of Henrietta Gordon stood there, the same smile on her face. "Should I scream right about now?" she squeaked.

"I hope you don't. People scream so much because of a ghost, it's become cliche. I've waited for you, Holly. I'm so glad you decided to take the job to clean my home." Henrietta gazed at Merlin, who cocked his head. "I love this fine gentleman with you. We've had some wonderful times while you've been out."

Holly glanced at her cat, who wasn't as innocent as he appeared to be. "Thanks, but how did you know I decided to come here? Aren't ghosts tied to wherever they haunt?"

"Pure fantasy. We can visit family, even if they don't live close by." Henrietta chuckled as she gazed at Holly. "I went to see Randolph. How do you think my brother knew to hire you? It took a little nudge to get him to do what I wanted." The ghost floated over to the window. "You are the one I've chosen to be the rightful heir to this house. Randolph's horrible daughter will never take my place. I banned both my brother and my niece from ever setting foot here."

Holly opened her mouth, then shut it. "I almost

asked how you knew he wanted his daughter here. If you already kind of contacted him, it makes sense you know his plans. I don't think I can get this place ready in thirty days anyway. Well, less than thirty days now. Your house is beautiful, but it's huge. I loved it the moment I stepped inside. I can picture what it must have been like to live here and have friends over or parties or be decorated for the holidays."

"I'm so happy to hear you say so. The house is large for a reason, which you'll discover soon enough. I suspect Raymond Burnett will take you to meet Delia Warner. He will be as important to the house as he will be to you. Delia should be able to give you some answers." Henrietta turned to her. "This house is very important to Garland Falls. If Lydia Gordon moves in here, it would spell disaster for the town."

"I don't understand. What would happen?"

"She and my brother both want the Master Key. Once you find it, you'll understand." The ghost stared out of the window. "My time is short. Remember what I told you."

"Where is the key? He told me to keep a lookout for it, but I haven't found it yet." Holly stared as Henrietta's form faded away. "Please, Henrietta. Tell me where to look for it."

The light faded and Holly woke up in bed. Merlin stared at her as she threw the covers off and hurried to the third floor. She ran to the door at the end of the hall and found it locked tight. "It couldn't have been a dream," she said. "It felt too real."

She tugged on the door one last time before she retreated back to her room. The cat had curled up at the foot of the bed and began to purr when she lay back down. "Merlin, I think I've gone crazy. Did you go with me to the upstairs room?" She frowned when he closed his eyes and ignored her question. "Thanks for the non-help. Good night, buddy."

****

Sunshine hit her in the face the next morning, and she rolled over and groaned. Sleep evaded her after she'd convinced herself she had a way too realistic dream. She didn't have time to be exhausted. She still had a lot to do downstairs and the upper floors still waited for her to get to them.

She'd seen a hardware store on Main Street and decided to go there to order the new kitchen appliances. She made a mental note to ask about a company to inspect and clean the chimney. She also needed a steam vac for the carpets. She pulled the covers over her head.

The bed felt a lot more comfortable than the list of chores creating chaos in her mind. If only there wasn't so much to do in such a short amount of time. She needed longer than thirty days to make the house perfect. Merlin walked up her body and meowed in her ear. She peeked out from the covers and frowned. He was nose to nose with her. Sometimes her buddy could be a real killjoy.

She dragged herself to the bathroom and splashed water on her face. She'd shower when she stopped for the day. As she dressed, she decided to go to the hardware store before she'd get to work. If she could get a steam vac, she could check one more task off the list of chores which grew by leaps and bounds every day. At least she'd started on the linens she'd found so far.

Time to get herself and Merlin some breakfast. She

stopped at the bottom of the third-floor staircase. She glanced up, then shook her head and went downstairs. Her mind wandered as she ate two pieces of toast. Last night's dream felt so real, but ghosts didn't exist, did they? With the strange doors and the weird keyring, she could believe anything at this point.

She grabbed her keys and drove to Main Street. She parked in front of the hardware store and hoped the owner could help her. The bell over the door rang and an older man came out from a back room.

"Good morning," he said. "I'm Lou. How can I help you?"

"Hi. My name is Holly Stevens. I've been hired to clean the large house on Darkling Street. I wondered if you knew where I can get new kitchen appliances. The ones in the house are a little out of date."

"I'd heard someone had been hired to do some work out there. Nice to meet you." Lou pulled a catalogue out from under the counter. "Let's see what we can find for you. How much is your budget?"

"Well, it's Randolph Gordon's money, so I don't want to be too extravagant. I'd like more up-to-date appliances. The refrigerator needs a definite replacement. It's got a funky smell. I don't think there's enough disinfectant on the planet to get rid of it."

"The ones on these two pages aren't too expensive and should meet your needs." He turned the page. "I think Randolph would approve."

Holly picked out what would be good for the house and its new occupant. "Also, do you know of a good company to inspect and clean the chimney? I think it would be a good idea to make sure it's in good working order."

"I know of a few people who can help. I'll call around and get you some prices." Lou sat on the tall stool behind the counter. "What else can I do for you today?"

"I think I covered the important items for now. I'm sure I'll be back soon. Thanks, Lou."

She turned back to the catalogue and made notes of what she wanted to purchase to tell Randolph how much she spent. She also wrote a reminder to herself to double check the light bulbs at the house so she could have replacements on hand. The bell over the door chimed.

She turned and smiled when she saw Ray. "Good morning. I didn't expect to see you this early."

"Me and the original bad penny. You never know where I'll turn up." He smiled at her. "I thought I saw your car outside. Lou, Lucas needs another three bags of potting soil. You have any left?"

"I think I have five bags in stock. You want them all?" He grinned when Ray nodded. "I haven't seen you in town this much in ages. Doesn't Lucas come in for supplies himself? I thought he kept you at the shop to take care of the customers. After all, everyone who goes there loves to talk to you."

"Yeah, that's the usual arrangement. However, his wife came back from her last assignment and has some vacation time. I get to do his errands so he can spend more time at home." He turned to Holly when Lou went to the back for the soil. "Can I buy you lunch today?"

"Thanks for the invitation, but I think it's time I buy you lunch." She flipped through the catalogue pages for a minute. "Why don't you come into town much?"

"You saw the reactions I get." He leaned against the counter and folded his arms. "I know how people here feel about me, so I stay away as much as possible. No point making the situation worse for everyone."

She held his hand and gave it a gentle squeeze. "I think you need to have someone with you who likes you for who you are. I don't care what people think. I like you and think you're a nice person. We'll show people how great you are, whether they like it or not."

"You don't know how much it means to know you support me, even though we've basically met a couple of days ago."

Lou came out with the five bags on a flat cart. "Are you parked out front?"

"Yeah. I'll bring the cart back in a minute. Lucas said to put these on his account and he'll be in later this week to settle up."

After Ray walked out, Holly turned to Lou. "Oh, I remembered what else I need. It's the main reason I came here. I could use a steam vac. The carpets are in good shape, but the dirt and dust are so ground in, my vacuum can't get them as clean as I'd like. You wouldn't happen to have one, would you?"

He smiled. "As a matter of fact, I do. It arrived yesterday. I knew I would need to have one on hand."

"What a lucky coincidence," she said. "Do these types of situations happen this often?"

"More often than you think. After you're here for a while, you won't even notice them. You'll just take them as they come."

He brought the steam vac around the counter and she wheeled it out to her car. Ray walked back out after he returned the flat cart and put it in the trunk of her car. She gazed at him and wanted to tell him about the weird dream, but it couldn't be said in a few minutes. She'd tell him at lunch.

"See you later," she said.

"Yeah. We both have work to do. I'll be by around noon."

As she drove back to the house, she couldn't wait for the morning to be done so she could see him again.

Chapter Eight

Holly checked the time on her phone with more and more frequency as she worked. The morning dragged on and no amount of wishing lunch time would arrive hurried the minutes any faster. She'd wait to use the steam vac until the afternoon. The carpets needed her full attention, unlike the mundane task of scrubbing the baseboards and floors. Distractions didn't matter when she worked on those areas.

She looked at her phone one more time and jumped to her feet. Time to get ready for her lunch date. Ray would be here in fifteen minutes. Dirty water emptied, rubber gloves thrown in the bucket, and now to hurry upstairs to put on clean clothes and neaten her hair. She'd like to be ready before he showed up for a change.

She reached the bottom step as he knocked. "Right on time," she said when she opened the door.

"I like to think punctuality is one of my better traits. Are you ready to go?"

"Yep." She slung her purse over her shoulder and locked the house. "You want to take your car or mine?"

He glanced over his shoulder. "Why don't we take yours. You offered to take me to lunch so I assumed you'd drive. After all, I think we could consider this a date, right?"

Her heart flip flopped in her chest at his

suggestion. "Of course, we'll consider this a date. I asked and you accepted. I think this qualifies as a date." She waved toward her car. "Your chariot awaits."

Holly glanced at him as she pulled out and guessed the real reason for his answer. He didn't want people to know he'd come into town until they saw him. She couldn't blame him for his desire to remain unnoticed. She couldn't imagine living in a town where you weren't wanted.

"Should we go to the diner again? You mentioned some other places to eat in town. We can go there if you like."

"The diner is fine. It's close and even when they're busy, the service is fast."

She reached over and gave his hand a brief squeeze. "You know, you don't have to worry about what people think when I'm with you. I'll tell them all where to go if they say one bad word to you."

"Have you appointed yourself my defender?"

"Yes, I have." She pulled into a parking space not far from the diner. "I'm your friend first and your defender second."

He took her hand as they walked to the diner. "I couldn't ask for a better friend or someone to defend me. Thank you, Holly."

They took a seat at the counter and ordered and smiled as Sally served everyone at her usual breakneck pace. As soon as they got their food, Holly turned to him. She didn't know where to start, but decided to jump right in.

"Last night, I had the weirdest dream. It felt so real, but I woke up in bed."

Ray ate in silence for a minute. "What happened in

it? Please tell me you didn't have the one where you think you can fly." He stared at her. "You didn't try to fly, did you?"

She smiled. "No, of course not, but one almost as strange. I saw a light under my door. I followed it up to the third floor and went through the door at the end of the hall. I'd never seen a bedroom so large. The ghost of Henrietta Gordon greeted me. She said she didn't want her niece in her house and claimed me as the rightful heir. She said she convinced her brother to send me here."

Ray frowned a little. "You're right. I've never heard of a dream like that. It could have been some kind of vision. Why would Henrietta's ghost want you to take over her house? Do you have any connection to the family?"

"I've never been told I have, so I don't think so. My mother did tell me once she had relations somewhere in the northern Midwest," she said. "When I woke up, I went upstairs and the door is locked. There's no way I could've been in the room, but I know I'd gone in there. I could see it so clearly. I picked up a picture, I felt the bedspread, but I know I couldn't have been in there."

"You need to talk to Dee Warner and maybe Mrs. Hall. They know a lot about the history of Garland Falls and about the families here."

They walked up to the register when they finished, to make room for other patrons. "Henrietta said you'd take me to Dee Warner. She also said you'd be important to the house and to me." She smiled as his cheeks turned pink. "I guess no one ever said so before, huh?"

"No." He looked up and then turned around. "We should leave. We both have work to do. I'll come by this afternoon and start on the yard. I'm sorry I haven't been able to get over there earlier. We got busy yesterday and I stayed late to help Lucas."

"We all know what kind of man you are, and I'm sure this young lady will find that out soon enough," Mayor Jacobs said behind him.

Ray took a deep breath and faced the mayor. "You of all people should know how busy we are when it gets close to time for Founders Day. It will be here in less than a month."

"When is Founders Day?" Holly asked. She suspected the end date coincided with her final date.

"September twenty-second, the autumnal equinox," Ray said.

She sighed. "Somehow, I knew you would say that. That's my end date for having the house done."

The mayor stuck his hand out. "I'm Mayor Jacobs. Who might you be?"

"Holly Stevens." She shook the mayor's hand. "I've been hired by Randolph Gordon to clean the house on Darkling Street. Ray has offered to help me with the yard work. He's so nice to offer and I'm grateful he can take time out of his busy schedule."

"Ms. Stevens, Ray Burnett is a lot of things, but I can't include nice on the list."

Holly narrowed her eyes. "I see. Did you even try to get to know him? No? You must be one of those people who judges first and then demands more proof before you accept a person." She got right up in his face. "I'll tell you right now, Mr. Mayor. I'll take ten Ray Burnetts to one of you. Now, if you'll excuse us, we have jobs to get back to. I suggest you do the same."

She grabbed Ray's hand and pulled him after her as she elbowed her way by the mayor and his cabinet members. The mayor and the town elders stood there and stared after them, their mouths hanging open. She unlocked the car and got in, and waited until Ray hooked his seatbelt. She turned the key, then let out the laugh she'd held in.

"Did you see their faces?" She turned to Ray, happy to see him smile. "I bet no stranger ever put them in their place before, did they?"

He shook his head. "The one person who argues with them is Mrs. Hall. I think they're a little used to her, though. Thank you. You didn't have to stand up to them for me."

"Yes, I did, and you can do it too, you know. You don't have to put up with how they talk to you or about you." She laid her hand on his leg. "Dig down deep and find the courage to tell them where to go when they talk to you like that. It's easier than you think."

He stared straight ahead. "I wish it were as simple as you make it sound. You see, I and my neighbors on Darkling Street, we have a kind of a, not reputation, but a stigma in Garland Falls. It's a black mark some of the town elders can't get over."

She pulled up in front of her house and turned the car off. "Can you tell me about it? Maybe I can help. After all, I'm a Darkling Street resident myself right now. I won't have people talk badly about my neighborhood."

"I think Henrietta's ghost came to the right conclusion. You are the best person to take over this house." He leaned over and kissed her cheek. "We've both got work to get back to. I'll be over this afternoon to start on the yard when I finish at the nursery."

"Great. I'll see you later."

They got out and Holly waved to Ray as he got in his car and drove off. She unlocked the house and walked inside. Merlin sat on the bottom step, as usual, to wait for her. She walked over and picked him up before she flopped on the couch.

"The mayor has a really bad attitude toward Ray and I don't like it," she said, as she scratched the cat behind his ear. "I think I need to help change some minds in this town. I don't know why people can't see Ray as a great guy." She laid her forehead on top of Merlin's head. "Henrietta did say he would be important. I believe he's become an important part of our lives, hasn't he?"

Merlin meowed before he jumped down. She sighed and stood. "Right. Time to get back to work. The days have started their countdown. September twenty-second will be here before we know it."

****

Ray finished re-potting snapdragons and dusted his hands off. "Lucas, can I ask you a random question?"

"Sure. What's on your mind?"

"Why did you give me a chance?" Ray put the tools back on the shelf. "A lot of people, and I mean people with pull here, don't like me and won't give me any kind of opportunity to prove myself. So, why did you?"

"Is this about what happened at the diner today?" Lucas smiled when Ray nodded. "It's already all over town how Holly put the mayor in his place after he insulted you in front of everyone. Have a seat and we'll talk for a minute."

When they both had pulled over stools, Lucas
leaned on the worktable. "I want you to believe what
I'm about to tell you. You're a good man, Ray. Yes,
you have a connection to the Dark Lands, but your
father isn't a bad person. Like everyone, he has a job to
do. I've been to the Dark Lands a lot and I've never had
any problems. We're all people. There are some
differences and maybe Dark Landers play a few more
tricks than most, and have more ties to forbidden
magic, but you don't."

"But I carry the capacity for darkness in me." Ray
drew circles in the spilled soil on the table. "What
happens if, or when, it comes out?"

"You'll still be my friend." Lucas sat back and
folded his arms. "You know I have my own ties to
magic and nature. I can see a person's heart and sense
their true selves. I hired you because I saw the problems
you had when you wanted a job in Garland Falls.
People who didn't know you, and didn't want to know
you, judged you based on who your father is. I never
want to be the person who turns his back on someone in
need. I got to know you. Whether the mayor likes it or
not, you're an important part of this town."

Ray nodded, grateful for Lucas' kind words.
"Holly said Henrietta's ghost told her I would be
important to her and the house. What do you think she
meant?"

"I don't know. Maybe Holly is the one for you."
Lucas stood and pushed the stool back under the
worktable. "Talk to Dee Warner. She might have an
idea."

"I already had a trip to the B and B planned." Ray

followed Lucas back to the shop. "You're a good friend, Lucas."

Lucas grinned. "Like my mother would let me treat anyone with any type of rudeness. Even though I'm a grown man and married, doesn't mean she wouldn't ground me and send me to my room. And she'd have my wife on her side, also."

They laughed as they went into the shop to begin preparations for the afternoon crowd.

Chapter Nine

Holly pulled the steam vac into the living room and set it up. She'd never used this model before, but the controls looked simple enough. The machine looked easier to operate than a lot of the others she'd used in the past. She pushed the furniture off the area rug and got to work.

Her thoughts turned to the mysterious key Randolph and Henrietta's ghost were concerned about. They both called it the Master Key. Would it make the ones on the keyring unlock the doors they matched? She didn't find it in the living room, so where could the mysterious key be? She didn't find it in the bedroom she'd chosen, as she'd cleaned the room when she moved in. Maybe the rolltop desk had a secret compartment. They did in the movies. Or would it be too cliché?

When she finished, the rug looked brand new. The runner in the hallway could stand to be cleaned too. She sighed. She'd have to clean all the carpets like this. Thankfully, it had taken less time than she figured it would. The only rugs downstairs were the area rugs in the living room and the study, and the runner in the hallway. All the bedrooms had carpets in addition to runners in the halls. Merlin stared at her through slitted eyes and yawned.

"Why are you tired when I do all the work, you

lazy cat?" She laughed when he answered with a loud meow. "We have a few more rooms down here, then we can move to the second floor. I'm glad the other rooms on this floor don't need as much work because time will be up before we know it and we've already come to the end of our first week. Most of it was working on the living room. We still have the study, the library, the dining room, and two bathrooms to finish on this floor."

In the kitchen, she poured out the dirty water and washed the tank. Soft music drifted to her and she paused. "Christmas music in August again? What is the deal with this house?"

She walked over to the green door at the back of the kitchen. She touched the knob, turned it, and jumped back when it opened. "Okay. This is freaky. How does a locked door open by itself? Even the door's key didn't open it." She glanced at Merlin who sat at her feet. "Should I freak out right about now?"

The cat lay down, tucking his front paws in.

"Thanks for the support."

Holly took a deep breath to steady her nerves and stepped through. Light tan wood paneling with Nordic designs lined the short hallway and she ended up in a large kitchen. Scents of cinnamon, vanilla, chocolate, and sugar made her mouth water. She turned as an older woman walked in carrying a tray laden with all types of pastries. Her light-blue shirt and tan pants had smudges of flour on them. An apron decorated with mistletoe and more flour was tied around her waist.

"Well, hello." The woman wiped her hands on her apron. "I'm Felicity Claus. You must be Holly Stevens. News about you has spread like wildfire through the fairy realms. There are a lot of people very curious about you."

"This isn't possible," Holly muttered as she rubbed her forehead. "There are fairy realms and they're curious about me?"

"Of course. Your magic is felt throughout the realms." Felicity laughed at the confused look on Holly's face. "You wouldn't believe how much is possible where magic is concerned."

"I mean, this door was locked. Even the key wouldn't open it." She stared at the older woman. "And you're Felicity Claus? As in Mrs. Santa Claus?" Holly staggered over to a chair and dropped onto it. "And you think I have magic? You know what? I think I've inhaled too many fumes. This is either another weird dream or I've started to have major amounts of hallucinations."

Felicity sat across from her. "There must be a reason why you're here. How can I help you?"

"Wake me up?" she said, as she gave Felicity a weak smile.

"I understand this is hard for you right now, but all will come clear in due time."

"Do you have any information about an antique brass key? It's important to a lot of people around me." She sighed and propped her chin on her hand. "Everyone calls it the Master Key. But the Master Key to what?"

Felicity stared at her for several minutes. "It's not for me to say. You'll find it when the time is right, and not before. Trust yourself and Ray Burnett. He may be the answer to all your questions."

"What?"

Holly blinked and found herself back at the kitchen

sink. Water spilled over the sides of the steam vac tank and she shut off the tap. Merlin sat on the counter, and his tail twitched as he watched her. Her phone buzzed in her back pocket, and she jumped.

"Hello? Oh, hi, Mr. Gordon. Yes, I've made good progress on the house. I ordered new appliances for the kitchen and they should be installed sometime next week. The living room took longer than I expected, but I should be back on track soon. I also looked into having someone to come check out and clean the chimney." She paused. "Yes, I'll have all the receipts for you. I can take pictures of them and send them to you. I've tried to keep expenses to a minimum. I don't want to take advantage of your generosity."

Another pause while he spoke. She nodded and smiled at Merlin. "Yes sir, I've kept my eye out for the key, but I haven't found it yet. I'm sure it'll turn up before long. I did find a keyring with thirteen keys on it. I know the other one is the one you want, though. I want to check the rolltop desk more tonight. As soon as I find it, I'll let you know." She waited again. "Yes, I'll call you when I find it, any time, day or night. Goodbye, Mr. Gordon."

She scratched her cat under his chin. "He's anxious to get the Master Key. I wonder what's so important about it?" Merlin licked her palm, and his rough tongue made her giggle a little. "I swear you have all the answers to this house. I wish you could tell me what you know."

She walked back over to the green door and turned the knob. She frowned when she found it still locked. How could she have gone through a sealed door? First the door upstairs, now this one. If the creepy purple door opened, she'd slam it shut and block it with the heaviest piece of furniture she could find. She had no desire to face whatever remained hidden behind that particular door.

"Strange things are afoot in this house, Merlin. I hope we find out the answers before we leave. I hate having an unsolved mystery." She refilled the tank and took it back to the steam vac. "We'll finish the rugs, then have another look at the desk."

****

Lucas snapped his fingers in front of Ray's face. "Hello? Are you in there?"

"What?" Ray blinked several times and shook his head. "Sorry, Lucas. I guess my mind went elsewhere for a minute."

"I can believe it. Does Holly still occupy your thoughts most of the time?"

Ray walked to the front of the store, locked the door, and flipped the open sign to closed. "She's always in my thoughts, but there's more to it than that. I felt like I walked with her through the North Pole door. I felt her confusion, but she wasn't frightened. Lucas, the longer she stays in the house, the more she's started to change. I can sense a different type of magic in her and it's growing in strength. This is different from all the other magics we've faced in Garland Falls."

"She can't be in danger. I'm sure you would've known right away if that were the case," Lucas said. "So far, she's met Henrietta's ghost, and from what you said, met Mrs. Claus. Maybe Garland Falls wants her to know about her magic. Maybe whatever magic she holds has woken up."

"But why would I feel and see what she does?"

"Because, my friend, I believe you two are connected on a deeper level than either one of you know." He wiggled his fingers at him. "I can sense it with my mystic powers."

"Lucas, you're a Green Man and you deal with nature. I don't think you were given 'mystic powers' by your ancestors."

"You never know." Lucas grinned and went into his office to finish the day's paperwork.

Ray thought about what Lucas said as he cleaned the store while his boss counted the money. It made sense, but how could he and Holly be connected when they'd met a week ago? His mother would say it didn't matter. Love sometimes didn't need any time at all to let two people know they were meant for each other.

"I'm done, Lucas. Mind if I take off? I told Holly I'd be over to start on the yard work around the house."

"Go ahead. I'll see you tomorrow."

Ray hurried out to his car. He drove to his house and parked and waved to Mrs. Lang as she watered her garden. He ran down to the large manor house, anxious to start, but more anxious to see Holly. He knocked on the door, a wide grin on his face when she opened it.

"I wanted to let you know I'm here. I'll check to see what needs to be done first. I'll have to go to my house and get some equipment, but it won't take me long."

"Sounds good." She chewed her lip for a minute, then blurted out, "I think I went to the North Pole today."

He took her hand and gave it a gentle squeeze. "I know. I think I went with you, in spirit."

"You saw it, too? Thank goodness. I didn't want to

think I went crazy." She glanced down at Merlin as he circled around their ankles. "And I'm pretty sure this guy knows all about this house, but I don't speak cat."

Ray winked. "Maybe you don't right now, but who knows what the future will bring." The tension in his shoulders eased when she smiled. "We can't stand here all day. I've got to get started on the yard. We'll get some dinner in a little while."

"Great. I should have enough time to finish the downstairs rugs and I want to examine the rolltop desk a little more. I found the keyring there, so I hope the antique key will be hidden on it somewhere."

"Good luck. I'll come get you when I'm done."

Ray walked down the steps and into the high grass. He might need the heavy mower from the nursery. The weeds were tall and thick, but dry and brittle. He found flower beds with three tiers overgrown with high weeds around the foundation. Those would take a lot of work to return them to their former glory. His fingers twitched with anticipation. He'd start with the gardens. He should mow the yard first, but he couldn't wait to work on the flower beds.

It might even be easier to mow once he found the edge of the gardens. He pulled his work gloves out of his back pocket and got to work. As he revealed more and more of the ground, the mayor's treatment of him retreated to the far reaches of his mind. Working with his hands eased his mind and his soul and he loved the hard work.

He always found joy as he gave some TLC to the areas which needed it. This work is what gave him purpose. He loved to take forgotten yards and gardens and make them beautiful again. Ray knew his boss understood his ability to find what it took to make unhealthy plants grow again.

The sun had started its descent when Holly appeared on the porch. "Wow. You've gotten a lot done in one afternoon. I can't imagine how great the yard would look if you had a whole day."

He used the back of his hand to wipe the sweat from his forehead. "Thanks. It helps that I love the work. Are you ready for dinner?"

"I am if you are." She glanced at herself, then him. "I think we both need a shower first. Come back in about thirty minutes and I should be ready."

"I'll be here all neat and tidy."

They stood there for a few extra minutes. They didn't speak, just gazed at each other. Ray broke the silence first. "I suppose we should get a move on. Be back in a few."

As he walked back to his house, he couldn't wait to get back to her. And if tomorrow played out as well as today, he would be in for a great week.

Chapter Ten

The next morning, Holly finally finished the living room. She had searched all through the rolltop desk after Ray had dropped her off after dinner. The large key still couldn't be found. She didn't think it would be there but looked anyway to make sure. She dusted the furniture and mopped the hardwood floor not covered by the area rug. The room glowed with life. The open windows let in the summer breeze which scented the room with aroma of the woods and flowers nearby.

Ray occupied her thoughts while she started on the study. They'd had a wonderful dinner, made better when the town elders were polite to them. They had made a point to talk to Ray without sarcasm or malice. They'd kept their comments civil and, some might even say, cordial.

She pulled out the metal plantstand and started to dust it. "Ouch!"

Holly snatched her hand back from behind the plantstand and stared at her hand. Blood had started to ooze from a long scratch on her palm. Her eyes watered as sharp pinpricks of pain started and her fingers twitched. She rose to her feet and hurried to the kitchen and stuck her hand under cold water. The water turned colder by the minute, but still the blood seeped from the cut.

Merlin jumped on the counter and lay down,

watching her tend to the wound. She smiled at him. "It's not serious, but I think that plantstand needs to go. It's dangerous. I didn't know the edges were so sharp. They didn't look bad. What a way to start the day."

Blood continued to leak out of the cut and she wrapped a towel around it. Out of all the supplies she packed, she couldn't believe she forgot her first aid supplies. She grabbed her car keys. "I'll be back in a little while, Merlin. Stay away from the plantstand. I think it's more dangerous than it lets on."

She got in her car and headed to Main Street. The general store should have some bandages and whatever else she might need. She blinked against the bright sun and searched for her sunglasses. She ground her teeth when they weren't where she'd left them. They had disappeared along with most of her patience for the morning.

She parked in front of the general store and walked in. The familiar aroma of popcorn, soap, and other items surrounded her. Pain spiked in her hand and shocked her back to the present. She looked around and spied the same older man as he stocked shelves, a stack of similar boxes next to him. She made her way over to him, the worn wooden floor creaking with every step.

"Excuse me," she said. "Can you help me?"

He rose to his feet and turned, a wide smile on his face. "Sure can. We didn't have a proper introduction the other night. I'm Mac, the owner of this store. You came in with Ray Burnett. What can I do for you?"

"Holly Stevens." The blood seeped through the thin dish towel as she held her hand out. "Do you have a first aid kit? I cut myself on a mean-spirited plantstand."

Mac unwrapped the towel and let out a quiet whistle. "You've got a nasty wound there. What did you put on it?"

She winced as he opened her hand a little more. "I don't have any first aid supplies. I ran it under cold water, but the bleeding won't stop."

Bells over the door chimed and they turned when Ray walked in. "Holly?" He hurried over to her. "What happened?"

"I cut myself."

Mac winked. "She got the cut from a mean-spirited plant stand."

"The Gordon house has a mind of its own." Ray held her hand in his own while he looked it over. "You might need stitches."

"Is there a doctor in Garland Falls? I didn't see an office here on Main Street."

Ray led her outside and helped her into his car. "We have a small hospital. They aren't too busy because not a lot of people here get sick. They should be able to fix you up."

As they drove the short distance to the hospital, Holly glanced at him. "What did you mean the house has a mind of its own? You know more than you want to share with me, don't you?"

"All I know are rumors. The manor has kind of a reputation. No one wants to enter it, but we all know it's important to the town." He helped her out of the car. "From the look of your hand, you might need my help more than ever now."

She looked at her hand and rolled her eyes. "I think you might be right. I hope this doesn't put me too far behind in my work. I'm halfway through my second week already."

They walked in and Ray stood with her at the counter while she checked in. She noticed how the nurse stared hard at Ray. From her narrowed eyes and deep frown, it was apparent the nurse wanted him gone. Animosity rolled off her in waves to crash against them.

"How did the cut happen?" the nurse asked.

"I cleaned a plantstand and didn't realize it had some sharp edges." She shrugged. "I certainly know better now."

"This stand didn't come from you, did it, Mr. Burnett?"

"What?" His gaze shot up to the nurse. "No. I went to Mac's to pick up some new plant stakes for the nursery and found Holly there. When she showed me the cut, I thought she needed to come here in case she needed a shot or stitches."

The nurse came around the counter. "Come with me, Ms. Stevens and we'll get you fixed up." She glared at Ray. "You can wait in here or outside; your choice."

Holly saw the hurt in Ray's eyes as she followed the nurse. He didn't kid her when he said some people in Garland Falls didn't like him. She couldn't believe how hostile the nurse had been. She sat quietly as the nurse, now all smiles and friendliness, took her vital signs and chatted.

"Why don't you like Ray?" Holly said.

The nurse put away the blood pressure machine and other items. "It's well known around town who his family is. You'd be wise to stay away from him. He'll cause you problems."

"But he's been so nice to me and he's helping me

with the yardwork around the Gordon house. I don't see how he could be a bad person. My cat loves him."

The nurse shrugged and picked up the paperwork. "Well, don't say I didn't warn you. The doctor will be here in a few minutes."

Holly glanced around the room as she sat on the bed. Pictures of flowers were on the walls, as well as schematics of human skeletons and some creatures who didn't resemble people at all. What kind of a doctor had these kinds of diagrams on an exam room wall? Maybe she made a mistake coming here. Between these pictures and the nurse's attitude toward Ray, nervousness soured her stomach and she swallowed hard. *I should leave. This place is too weird, even for a hospital.*

She started to get up when the doctor walked in. He had sandy-brown hair and pale-blue eyes. He smiled at her and laid the paperwork on the counter. "I'm Dr. O'Brien. Tell me what brings you in here today, Ms. Stevens."

"I cut my hand while I cleaned a plantstand. I'm glad it had dust on it and not rust. I'd hate to have to get a tetanus shot. I always have a lot of pain with those. I rinsed the cut out with cold water, but the blood wouldn't stop." She paused to gauge the doctor's reaction. "Ray Burnett brought me. He thought I should have a doctor look at it."

O'Brien unwrapped her hand and examined it. "He made the right call. Ray's a good man."

"Your nurse doesn't have the same impression as you. She doesn't like him."

He smiled. "Alesia doesn't like a lot of people, but she's a good nurse." He murmured to himself for a few minutes as he studied the wound. "The bleeding stopped, so I don't think you need stitches. I've got some medicine I can put on it. It's an herbal salve people swear by. Keep it covered for a few days and you'll be good as new."

"Thanks, Dr. O'Brien."

He tended to the cut, then escorted her out. "Remember to come back if it starts to look infected or if it causes you any more pain."

"I will." She waved to Ray. "Dr. O'Brien got me fixed up."

Ray walked over and shook the doctor's hand. "Nice to see you again, Sean. I didn't know you'd come back to Garland Falls."

"My dad retired and wanted me to take over here." He grinned. "You know no one says no to my dad, not even me."

"I'm glad you're back." He glanced at Holly. "Are you sure she's okay?"

"She'll be good as new in a couple of days." He leaned close and mock whispered, "I used my special salve on it."

Ray grinned. "I don't know what it is, but it does work wonders." He put his arm around Holly's shoulders. "Let's get you back to your car so you can get back to the Gordon house."

She stared at him through narrowed eyes for a moment. "You know, it's quite a coincidence how you turn up at the stores the same time I'm there."

He glanced at her and smiled. "Maybe it's fate and we're supposed to meet up all the time."

"I'm okay with your explanation. I think fate and I are on good terms at the moment."

They were quiet as he drove them back to Main Street. She turned and smiled at him. "I don't care what people think about you. I like you, Ray, very much." She glanced back at the hospital. "I think I need to have some words with his nurse, though. I didn't like her attitude toward you at all."

"It's okay, Holly. Let it go. Sean's said on numerous occasions, she doesn't like a lot of people. I try not to let her nastiness get to me."

"You're a better man than I am."

She gazed at him. She thought him a better man than a lot of people in Garland Falls.

Chapter Eleven

She got out of her car as Ray pulled up behind her when they got back to Darkling Street. He walked over and laid his hand on her arm. "Try not to use any strong cleansers today, okay?"

"Believe me, I won't. I know how bad those can hurt a deep cut." She slammed the car door shut. "I'm glad I scrubbed a lot yesterday, because it won't happen today. Can you come in and remove the plantstand? It's too dangerous and I don't want Merlin to get cut on it."

"And it already gave you one battle scar. You don't need any more."

He walked her up to the house and waited as she unlocked the door. As soon as she pushed the door open, Merlin ran to her and jumped in her arms. His ears were flat against his head and his body shook.

"Poor baby," she said as she cuddled him close to her chest. "What scared you so much?"

"Stay here," Ray said. "I'll go make sure there aren't any problems."

As he approached the purple door under the staircase, Merlin shot out of Holly's arms and blocked his steps as he hissed at the door. Ray knelt down and laid his hand on the cat's head. "It's okay, buddy. I have no desire to open the door. I know what's back there."

Holly came up behind them. "I found a keyring and

they have the same emblems as some of the doors. The keys don't open the doors, but it looks like my dreams do. This door makes its key act, I don't know, weird is the best way to describe it."

Ray stood and turned to her. "You didn't open this door, did you?"

"I tried, but then a strange thing happened. The key turned and I heard the lock click, but the door wouldn't open. Then, it felt like someone on the other side held the key and then the door vibrated like someone ran into it. What's the deal, Ray?"

He laid his hands on her shoulders. "I can't tell you, but promise me you won't ever open this door."

"I can promise I will never open this door." She removed his hands and held them. "I want you to tell me what you know about the Gordons and their house. What have I gotten myself into?"

"All I'll say for now is you'll have all your answers when the time is right."

"I hear the same line from a lot of people." She harrumphed and folded her arms while she stared at him. "I don't do cryptic statements. You'll have to do better."

"I said I'd take you to meet Dee Warner. I'll take you there tomorrow and let Lucas know I'll be in a little late. I mean, the sooner you talk to her, the better, and she might have some answers for you. It's not my place to tell you what you want to know." Ray walked to the living room and picked up the plantstand. He examined it and smiled. "I can sand down the sharp edges and re-paint it if you want. I'm glad it's white. I already have cans of white paint at the shop."

"Nice change of subject." she said. Then she

grinned and shrugged. "And if you can tame the mean metal beast, have at it. If it's the same color, I won't have to tell Mr. Gordon it bit me."

He winked. "You got it. Should I pick you up when I get off work? We can go get some dinner."

"Sounds wonderful. I can't buy groceries until the new appliances arrive. Lou said they should be here by the weekend. Around six or six thirty sound good?"

"Perfect. I'll see you then." He waved as he took the plantstand to his car.

****

Holly shut the door behind him and leaned against it. The effort to work on this house had become more than she bargained for. First, she'd been given an almost impossible deadline. Then the weird keyring and a door that led who knew where, and now her hand had been cut.

"Merlin, I think Mr. Gordon got out cheap with what he promised to pay."

The cat meowed his agreement.

She pushed off the door and grabbed some rubber gloves. "Time to get back to work."

Holly finished her work on the living room and made sure to keep a lookout for the antique key Mr. Gordon wanted her to find. The last thing to do was scrub the bricks around the fireplace until the natural red shone through. She'd had to empty the bucket three times to get clean water. The bricks were dirtier than she realized.

The study hadn't taken her long at all to clean. Henrietta must not have used that room too often. She pulled down the rest of the curtains on the first floor and took them to the laundry room at the back of the house. Those appliances looked like they'd seen better days. She may have to see how much it would be to replace those, too.

In the living room, she eyed the tall windows and groaned before she grabbed her stepstool. While she waited for the water to heat, she pulled on a pair of tight vinyl gloves, then pulled the rubber gloves back over them. With the bucket full of hot water, she picked up her scrub brush and got to work on the windows. Thin wood divided the windows into nine smaller panes, and there were four of those large windows. When these were done, the living room would be finished.

"Not only do the Gordons like leather furniture, they also like a lot of windows," she said to Merlin, who had perched on the back of the couch to watch her. "We've been here for almost two weeks. As much as I've done, it looks like I haven't even made a dent in this disaster."

She refilled the bucket three more times. Her high standards were met when the sun's rays formed diamonds of light on the floor. Merlin head butted her shoulder when she leaned against the couch. "You're right. I need to ask Ray for more help with the inside stuff. Maybe I can help him with the yard." She looked around the room and groaned, but she was glad she finished it. "I so need to take the 'no job too big or too small' off my website. This room by itself proved I have my limits after all."

Merlin swatted her pocket where she'd stuffed her cell phone. She pulled it out and looked at the time. "Wow. Almost six. Time sure does fly when you have way too much to do. Let's get ready. Ray will be here soon."

****

"Lucas, do we have any sandpaper?" Ray called from the back of the shop. He looked up when his boss walked outside. "I told Holly I'd smooth out the edges on this plantstand. It gave her a pretty nasty cut."

"I think I still have some in the house. Be right back."

Ray turned the stand around to examine every inch of the offensive item. He ran his fingers carefully over the edges of the leaves and vines which made up the base. He couldn't feel any sharp edges and wondered how Holly had cut herself.

"You look puzzled," Lucas said. He handed him the sandpaper as he leaned over Ray's shoulder. "Is there a problem?"

"I can't feel any edges sharp enough to cut someone." He looked at Lucas as the other man squatted down. "What do you think?"

Lucas ran his fingers around the edges, too. "You're right. There aren't any sharp edges. Are you sure this is the stand she said cut her?"

"She pointed right at it and told me to take it. Shouldn't there be blood on it somewhere?"

Both men stared at the stand and turned it in slow circles to check every inch. "I don't know what to tell you, Ray. This stand is fine."

Ray picked up the sandpaper. "Well, I told her I'd sand it down and re-paint it, so that's what I'll do."

"Maybe Henrietta's ghost wanted to throw you two together some more." Lucas grinned at Ray as he worked on the plantstand. "What time did you say you'd pick her up tonight?"

Ray's cheeks heated as he concentrated on the

stand. "Between six and six thirty. She doesn't have any food in the house yet." He paused and looked up at his boss. "She found the keyring and the door to the Dark Lands. She wanted to know if the house had any weird problems."

Lucas stood quiet for a moment. "What did you say about it?"

"I told her I didn't know much so I'd take her to Miss Dee. She always knows what to say to, let's call them, awkward questions."

"Good idea. Miss Dee will know how to handle this."

Ray worked on the stand, all the while his thoughts turned Holly. He didn't like the fact she stayed by herself in the Gordon house with only her cat to keep her safe. However, Henrietta's ghost had begun to look out for her. Not only did Garland Falls have magic, it also spawned mountains of questions, too. Who knew when the doors would want to be opened. Most opened into safe realms, but the Dark Lands were a whole other story.

Sure, he could guide her through the lands, but he'd been forbidden to return. His vision blurred for a moment and he sanded the stand harder. If it weren't for the Callahan brothers and a handful of other people in Garland Falls, he wouldn't have a friend anywhere. Oh, he could count on his mother to visit, but his father had to stay in the Dark Lands to try to keep situations there on an even keel.

Holly said she liked him "very much." She'd had no idea how grateful he'd been to hear those words. He liked her a lot, too. Maybe when she finished her work at the Gordon house, she'd be like some of the other people and stay in Garland Falls. Maybe, she'd even want to stay with him. As soon as the thought hit him, ugly taunts from his childhood slammed into his mind. No one ever wanted to be anywhere near him. Not until Holly came to Garland Falls.

His half-blood heritage had marked him as an outsider all his life. His father belonged to the hierarchy of the Dark Lands. His name? Strife, second to his uncle, Despair. His mother came from the Light Side and worked with Nature as a member of her court. And here he stood, the product of both and accepted by neither side. His parents loved him, but not any of his other relations. When people in Garland Falls found out his parentage, they either grudgingly accepted him or were outright hostile.

If he told Holly his true nature, would she still like him? He hoped so. He got the sense she would accept him faster than people who had known him longer. She did stand up to the mayor and his cronies for him. If he hadn't fallen for her before, he did right then.

He brought one of the smaller paint cans over, opened it, and dipped his brush in. He'd let the paint dry overnight and take it to her tomorrow. Right now, he had enough time to get ready for their dinner date. He'd never looked forward to eating out so much in his life.

Chapter Twelve

Holly hurried down the stairs when the bell rang and smoothed her hair. She took a deep breath and opened the door. Ray stood there with a small bouquet of flowers.

"I got these for you," he said as he held them out.

She held them to her nose and inhaled the sweet aroma. "Thank you, Ray. They're beautiful. Come on in while I find a vase to put them in."

She walked into the kitchen and Ray followed her. As she opened different cabinets, Merlin sauntered in and pawed at the pantry door. She opened it and found the perfect vase.

"Merlin knows this house better than I do." She filled the crystal vase and arranged the flowers. "And I'm not sure how, unless he lived here in another life."

"Cats do have nine lives, so you never know." He leaned down to scratch Merlin behind his ears "They also have a sixth sense about their environment. This guy knows a lot more than he wants to let on." Ray scratched Merlin under the chin and a loud purr filled the kitchen. "You know I'm right, don't you, buddy?"

Merlin meowed and rubbed his head against Ray's leg.

As they headed for the front door, a loud clang came from the living room. They looked at each other and walked in to see the large keyring on the floor once again. Holly stared at it, then shrugged and picked it up. The keys vibrated stronger in her hands, and she dropped them on the floor and backed away. This was their strongest reaction yet. She glanced at Ray. Could he be the reason? Henrietta did say he would be important to the house. And me, a tiny voice inside her said. Don't forget me.

"What's the matter?" Ray said. He watched Merlin go over and sniff the keys before he sat and stared at the two of them. "Does Merlin think there's a problem with those?"

"When I picked them up, they vibrated, almost like they were alive. There's no way they could have fallen on the floor. I put them back in the roll-top desk and shut it." She stared at the desk. "How can it be open now?"

"Maybe the catch is broken. Would you like me to take a look when we get back from dinner?"

She laid her hand on his arm and savored the strength she felt there. "I can't ask you for any more help. You've spent a lot of time and money on me, and I haven't even been here a full two weeks yet." She gave him a small smile. "And you did a lot on the yard yesterday."

Ray smiled and covered her small hand with his larger one. "It's not a problem. I wouldn't offer if I didn't want to do it."

She turned and gazed at him. "You've been so nice to someone you hardly know."

"I could say the same about you. Put the keys back and let's go eat." He looked around the now spotless living room. "You've done a lot of work. You must be hungry."

"Wow. I noticed I was hungry when *you* noticed I was hungry. I haven't eaten all day."

She took a deep breath and picked up the keyring. No vibrations; it didn't pull toward any doors. She blew out the breath she'd held. It behaved like an ordinary keyring. She put it in one of the small drawers in the desk's cubby hole and closed the rolltop. If the closed drawer and rolltop didn't keep them in there, nothing would.

They arrived at the diner in the middle of the dinner rush. They grabbed the last two seats at the counter. Ray turned quiet when the man next to him got up and left. Holly squeezed his hand and smiled. He nodded and looked up when Sally came over with menus.

"What'll it be tonight, you two?" She plunked two glasses of water down in front of them. "You've become a steady pair in here." She leaned closer to Ray. "Don't worry about the old fool who left. He doesn't like anyone."

"Thanks, Sally, but I know why he got up. I'm fine, really."

She raised an eyebrow. "If you say so."

"What's good tonight?" Holly asked. "The whole menu sounds delicious and I can't make up my mind."

"We've got a nice spaghetti with meatballs and garlic bread."

Ray and Holly looked at each other and grinned. "Sally, I don't know how you do it. It sounds perfect as usual," Ray said.

She picked up the menus. "It's a gift."

Holly watched more people walk away from where Ray sat and they wouldn't speak to her either. She didn't care. She had a short time to be in Garland Falls and if she could be his friend while she was here, she would. Why did she think being friends wouldn't be enough? Why did she suddenly want to be more than friends?

"You look deep in thought. Care to share?" he said.

"I can't get over how everyone treats you with such contempt," she said as she moved her silverware around. "It's so unfair to you. I may stay in Garland Falls longer to set some attitudes straight."

"I'm used to it. It doesn't bother me as much as it used to." He paused, then turned to her. "It would be nice if you did stay longer."

She nudged his shoulder with her own. "I'm happy to be here, but you, sir, are a terrible liar. I can see how much it hurts you every time."

"Thanks. I do have some friends here like Sally, the Callahans, Mrs. Hall, and Miss Dee." After they ate, Ray walked her down to the Heavenly Bites cookie shop. "Let me introduce you to a couple more."

Ray waved to a woman with short brown hair as she wiped down the counter. "Hi, Joanna. I'd like you to meet Holly Stevens."

Joanna tottered out from behind the counter and arched her back. "Nice to meet you, Holly. I hear you're the one who got picked to work on the Gordon house." She rubbed her very round belly. "Let's grab a seat. This whole pregnancy thing wears a person out."

Ray pulled a chair out for her. "Is Davin all right? Last time I saw him, he shook more than trees in a storm."

"He's been better, but I tell him this is all natural. Every time he starts to worry, I send him to Miss Dee's.

She's got a way to calm him down." She smiled. "If he thinks the pregnancy is bad, wait until the baby gets here. He'll be a basket case before long."

Holly laughed. "My friend back home said the same thing. Her husband worried more than she did."

Joanna arched her back. "So, what can I do for you two?"

"Holly's worried I don't have any friends here," Ray said.

Joanna nodded as she turned to Holly. "I noticed the coolness to Ray when I moved here. He's got lots of support from people who know the real him."

"I'm glad." Holly held Ray's hand. "He's offered to help me work on the house and I accepted." She held up her bandaged hand. "Especially now. I had a run-in with a nasty plantstand."

"You help her with whatever she needs, you hear me?" Joanna said. "We don't need the house to give her any more problems when she's alone."

"I'll be with her as often as I can," Ray said. "I do have to go to work and she has a fierce protector." When Joanna arched an eyebrow, he grinned. "Her cat, Merlin."

A tall man with white-blond hair came out from the back, a large box in his arms. "We got another baby present. How do you feel, Jo? You're not too tired, are you?"

"I'm fine, Davin. You can put it with the other gifts." She closed her eyes when he kissed the top of her head. "Ray brought Holly Stevens in to meet us. Randolph Gordon hired her to clean his sister's house."

"Nice to meet you, Holly." He shook Ray's hand. "Glad to see you back in here, Ray. It's been too long since we talked." He went to the case and came back with a box of cookies. "Consider this a welcome gift."

Holly took the box and set it on the table. "Thank you, Davin. Ray brought me some cookies from here on my first day. They were awesome."

Ray stood and Holly followed his example. "We'd better hit the road. I'm sure you two want to lock up and Joanna looks like she could use some rest."

Holly shook Joanna and Davin's hands. "I need to get back to the house and get some more work done. I'm glad to have met you. I'm sure I'll be back."

"We look forward to seeing you again, Holly," Davin said.

Ray drove them back to the Gordon house. As they walked up to the porch, he said, "I don't like the fact you have to stay here by yourself."

She opened the front door. "I don't have a choice." She reached to pet Merlin as he trotted out from the living room. "Merlin and I will be fine and you said you're right down the street. If there's any time I have a problem, I'll yell so loud, the whole town will hear me."

"I'll keep my windows open." He followed her in. "It's too dark to do any more outside. So, where should we start?"

"If you can start the dining room, I'll start on one of the bathrooms. Between the two of us, we should make some serious progress." She handed him half of her supplies. "Oh, and keep an eye out for a large, brass antique key. Mr. Gordon says it's important."

"Will do."

They went to their jobs and got to work.

Chapter Thirteen

The next day, Ray picked up Holly and drove up the hill to Warner's Bed and Breakfast. "Miss Dee knows a lot about the town, and she should have some answers for you about the Gordons and their house," he said.

Holly stared at the three-story Victorian home as she got out. "This place is about the same size as the house on Darkling Street, but this one has a much better vibe."

He escorted her to the front door. "It's all due to Miss Dee. You'll see when you meet her."

"Are you sure she's not too busy? Running a place like this must take a lot of her time. I wouldn't want to intrude."

Ray opened the front door. "She's got plenty of help. She hired someone this past winter and her nieces help out when she needs them." He waved to a short woman who wore a deep-blue carnation in her silver hair. "Hi, Miss Dee. This is Holly Stevens."

Dee Warner hurried around the mahogany desk and shook Holly's hand. "It's so nice to meet you. The whole town has talked about how Randolph Gordon wanted to get the house ready for his daughter."

"Yes, ma'am. Randolph Gordon hired me to clean it. Ray offered to help me with the yard and the higher stuff inside. It's a way bigger job than I expected."

"Call me Dee. Everyone does." She walked to the dining room and they followed her. "I took some cinnamon rolls out of the oven a few minutes ago. We'll eat and talk." When they were settled, Dee poured them all a glass of lemonade, then leaned on the table. "What would you like to know?"

Holly glanced at Ray, who smiled at her. "Why does everyone in this town have a problem with Mr. Gordon's daughter? When I bring it up, people look shocked, like they can't believe anyone from his side of the family would want to be here."

"Has Randolph's girl contacted you about how soon it will be done?" Dee asked.

"Not yet, but he's in a hurry to get the house ready. He gave me thirty days to fix it up and I've barely scratched the surface. I have a few more rooms left on the first floor, but two of them are bathrooms. Ray started on the yard and he helped me last night. I still have two more floors and an attic. I hope they don't need as much work as the living room did. It took almost the whole first week to do."

Dee smiled. "Don't worry. You'll get it done in no time."

"I thought you might be able to give Holly some history of the Gordons and why the house is important," Ray said. "She has a lot of questions you can answer better than me."

Dee sat back and rubbed her chin as she considered how to answer. "There's a lot to tell, but I'll try to hit the highlights. The Gordons were one of the original families of Garland Falls. Their house sat alone on Darkling Street for many years. It passed down through the family until Henrietta and Randolph were the last ones left. Randolph never cared for Garland Falls, but Henrietta loved it here. Everyone found Henrietta to be a lovely person, though she kept quiet and to herself. We all thought it a shame her husband left her when they couldn't have children."

"Ray hinted she had a bad fight with her brother. Randolph did tell me he hadn't seen his sister in years," Holly said. "Ray also said he didn't even show up for her funeral when she passed away."

Dee nodded. "We all thought he'd come back to live in the manor, but we never saw him after he left town. Rumor had it Henrietta banned him from her house. I hear he's a big shot now in New England."

"Yes, ma'am, he is." At Dee's smile, Holly corrected herself. "I mean, Miss Dee. He's got offices all over the place. Not sure what he does, but he makes a lot of money. He's one of the richest men in Vermont."

Dee sipped her lemonade. "After Henrietta's death, the town elders were sure he'd come back to take over the house, but he handled all his business through lawyers. I think he took his sister's words to heart. Then the place sat empty for seven years, and now you're here. I'm sure you'll breathe some life back into the house. It's far too gloomy out there on its own."

"I opened the windows, and it made a big difference in the atmosphere. It feels better in there already." Holly paused and ran her finger down the side of the sweating glass. "I found a keyring with thirteen keys. All the keys have symbols which match some of the doors on the ground floor of the house. Would you have any information about those?"

Dee and Ray exchanged a quick look. "Henrietta

never told me about keys. They must be important to the house, though. Do they unlock any of the doors?"

"I tried and the locks will turn but the doors don't open. It's strange, and the purple door under the stairs upsets my cat all the time. He won't let me go near it."

"Sounds like a smart cat," Dee said.

"He is," Ray chimed in. "Merlin is extraordinary. He even stopped me from getting too close to it."

"Cats have more smarts than a lot of people." Dee refilled their glasses. "What else can I tell you?"

"Why don't people here like Ray?" She smiled at him and squeezed his hand. "He's been so kind and helpful. And he sure knows how to feed a girl."

Dee chuckled. "Some prejudices can't be explained. Ray, why don't you go talk to Parker. We need some more variety with the flowers for the rooms and for outside."

He stood. "I think I've been dismissed. I'll be back in for you in a little bit."

After they heard the front door close, Dee moved over near Holly. "Ray has a dark lineage. I can't tell you all I know, but I can say he's a fine man. People are civil to him because of his mother. His father isn't welcome here, but I've never had a problem with him." She took Holly's hands. "I believe you're the person he needs to find acceptance in Garland Falls."

"How do you know? I'm here for such a short time. I'm not sure how big a difference I can make."

"Because, dear child, you have a strength in you and a strange, powerful magic surrounds you." Dee looked at her and smiled. "And I think you'll be here longer than you expect."

Holly stared at Dee. "If I have powerful magic,

how come I clean other peoples' houses for a living?"

"Because your magic shines as you work. You fill homes with love and light and laughter. When Ray works with flowers, he imbues them with the same strong emotions. You and Ray are a perfect complement." She winked. "You'll see. Now what else do you want to know?"

Holly sat quietly for a moment and thought about what Dee had said. She made a quick decision to change the subject. "Mr. Gordon told me to search for a large, brass antique key. Do you know why it would be so important to him?"

Dee frowned a little. "A large key," she murmured. "So, it's true. He doesn't have it."

"What?"

"We've all heard rumors of a Master Key in the Darkling Street house. The house has an important purpose in Garland Falls and that key figures into it." Dee sat up straight and smiled. "When you find the key, be sure to let Ray know. I can't tell you why right now, but don't tell Randolph you have it until we speak again."

"Okay," Holly said, drawing her words out. "What's the problem with Randolph Gordon? No one likes him much."

"He's a complicated person. We all thought Henrietta feared him. At least it looked that way from the outside. He'd been a hard man, always demanded his own way. Loud arguments between the two could be heard most nights. This all happened before the town grew to what it is now."

"But why? What would start these fights?"

"We didn't know." Dee stood and began to gather

the dirty dishes. "Some of the town elders suspected he became enraged because Henrietta wouldn't give him the key. After one last big fight, she threw him out of the house and told him to never come back."

"Wow. Pretty harsh of one sibling to ban the other." Holly got up and helped Dee take the dishes to the kitchen. "And he's never come back to Garland Falls since then?"

"No, and a lot of people were glad. Most of the town feared him." She took Holly's hands again and gave them a quick, firm shake. "He's not a man you want to disappoint, but please Holly, do *not* give him the key."

"I promise I'll come to you and Ray first." Holly watched Dee wash up the few dishes, then said, "Henrietta's ghost came to me in a dream, or maybe it was a vision. It makes my brain hurt to try and figure it out. She claimed she wanted me to be the rightful heir to her house. Would you care to comment on what she said?"

Dee dried the dishes and stacked them in the cabinet. "I'd heard rumors Henrietta's ghost still wandered her house. It's possible she waited for you to come. I'm sure you'll figure it all out when the time is right."

"I've heard this same statement before." She picked at a loose thread on her shirt. "As a matter of fact, it's what I hear from almost everyone."

"If everyone says it, then I'm certain it's true." She handed Holly a bag. "I put two cinnamon rolls in here for you, as well as some treats for your cat. I may come down to visit him. Let's go find Ray. You have a lot of work to do."

They walked out to the front porch and Holly looked around. She spied Ray as he talked to a tall man with tawny hair. "Is Ray's boss here? Shouldn't he be at his store?"

"No. That's Lucas' brother, Parker. He's my groundskeeper," Dee said. "Those boys look a lot alike, but their personalities are as different as night and day."

Holly waved to Ray, who walked over. "Have you two ladies finished your discussion about me?"

"We talked about Randolph Gordon a lot more, but yes, you were talked about," Holly said. "We couldn't say one bad word about you. Randolph Gordon, however, was another story."

"I'm glad to hear I'm on the good side of your conversation. You ready to get back to work?"

"Sure am. Time has slipped away too fast for me. My second week it almost up."

Dee hugged them both. "I'll see the two of you again soon. Holly, will you stay for the Founders Day celebration?"

"Unless a miracle happens and I get the house done in the next two and a half weeks, I'll be here. I haven't been to a party in ages. I work way more than I should."

"Wonderful. Then I'll see you there."

As Ray drove them back to Darkling Street, Holly stared out the window. "The town sure looks festive. There are so many colors, it looks like a rainbow dyed the town."

"Mrs. Hall is in charge of all the town festivities. She loves to put the events together and she goes all out every time. She's what some people refer to as a real ball of fire."

Holly grinned. "Maybe I should ask her to help me

clean the Gordon house."

"And don't think she wouldn't do it." Ray laughed. "She's wanted to get the place cleaned up for years."

He pulled up in front of the house and took the plantstand out of the trunk. "I tamed this beast, so it shouldn't bite you anymore. I'll be back later to continue with the yard. I've got to get to work."

"I'm glad you got it tamed," she said as she looked it over. "Thanks for taking me to meet Miss Dee today. She's a wonderful person and her cinnamon rolls are, too. She gave me a couple we can share when you come back."

"Since you've got dessert taken care of, I'll take care of dinner."

As Holly gazed at him, words stuck in her throat, keeping the word goodbye a prisoner. "Okay," she finally said. "I'll see you tonight."

She stood on the sidewalk, bag in hand, and watched him turn around and drive away.

Chapter Fourteen

Holly stepped into the house and Merlin made a beeline for her and jumped into her arms again. "I promise not to leave you alone so long, buddy. This house has freaked you out." A loud creak sounded from the second floor and her gaze shot to the ceiling. "Of course, I'm freaked out, too."

She put Merlin on the floor and started up the stairs, the cat right behind her. Another creak froze her on the steps. "Why am I doing this?" she mumbled. "You'd think I'd learn from all the movies I've watched. If there's a weird noise, never check it out alone."

Merlin meowed from behind her.

"You're right. All we have is us. Let's go." She climbed the steps and cringed at every squeak and groan. "It's the house, that's all. At least it better be the house," she mumbled as she continued up to the second floor. "Maybe Henrietta is restless and needs to walk around. Having a ghost here is kind of fun."

She opened the first door she came to and looked around the room. Empty. She proceeded down the hall, and opened every door to check every room, including the one she had taken. "We don't have time for this, Merlin. Why does this place have to have so many rooms?" Another creak sounded from the third floor. "If I hear a noise in the attic, you can bet I will not go up there until Ray comes back. Let's check out the third floor."

She walked back to the stairs and continued up and tried to be quiet and quick at the same time. The third floor only had six rooms, thank goodness, and no one jumped out at her when she opened four of the doors. The one door at the far end, she knew, led to the attic.

As she shut the last door, a flash of light caught her attention. She turned and at the other end of the hall, a white door with a large key carved into it stood sentry, as if to guard the secrets in the room beyond. She stood still and stared at the door. She took a hesitant step and swallowed hard. All she had to do was walk down and turn the knob. The door would be locked and she could go downstairs and get back to work.

As she approached, the white shimmered with all the colors of the rainbow. First white, then like an iridescent cloth, the white changed into blue, red, gold, green, orange, and purple. Holly frowned and leaned closer. The colors shimmered one more time, then they settled back into white. This house got stranger all the time. She took a deep breath and tried to stop trembling.

"This is the door I went through in my dream. Of course, it didn't look like this at the time. It looked like an ordinary door." Merlin meowed and she looked down at him. "We both know what's behind this, don't we? It's Henrietta's bedroom."

As she traced the lines, the rainbow light followed her finger. What did the symbol mean? Did the mysterious antique key go to this door? What kind of weird paint would make white not look like white? Merlin stood on his hind legs, stretching up on the door, and almost reached the carved brass knob. Holly took a deep breath and turned the knob, not surprised when the door didn't open. After she touched the door, the creaks and groans stopped.

"Well, buddy, this is a mystery for another day. I think we'll get in there when Henrietta wants us to. We'll show Ray when he comes over tonight. Let's get to work. With his help, we should be finished with the downstairs today. Let's get a jump on it."

After one more glance at the white door, Holly walked downstairs as Merlin scampered ahead of her. She stepped into the living room and found the keyring on the floor again. "Okay, house, I get it—they're important. You need to stop throwing these on the floor. I don't want to pick them up all the time." She put the keys back into the rolltop desk and shut it. "Now, stay put."

The whole time Holly worked on the ground floor her thoughts returned to the white door. Did the Master Key belong to the door upstairs? If she found it, would it open the door? The other keys didn't open their doors, so why should the one upstairs be any different?

What did Miss Dee mean about her being surrounded by powerful magic? She found Dee to be a pleasant lady, but she had a definite strange side. How could she help Ray find acceptance? Why did Dee insist she had powerful magic in her? The biggest question of all—why did she agree to come here in the first place? Clean a house and leave. No one told her about weird doors, magic, and one man who turned out to be more handsome than any man had a right to be. Okay, she loved the last one, but the rest she could live without.

She went to the kitchen and refilled her bucket with

clean water. She set it down when her phone buzzed in her back pocket. "Hello, Mr. Gordon. I planned to call you at the end of the week." She paused. "No, sir. I haven't found the key yet. I know I've been here almost two weeks. Yes, the keyring I found is still in the rolltop desk. I'll make sure to leave them there." Another pause. "Yes, sir. I'll keep you posted on my progress. The new appliances should be here this weekend and a company contacted me about coming out on Monday to work on the chimney. I think it will all be good by the time your daughter wants to move in."

She reached down to scratch Merlin while Mr. Gordon spoke. "Yes, sir. The company is local and Lou at the hardware store said they are very reputable and have good prices. Would you like me to take a picture of the receipts and text them to you? Sure, no problem. Thank you again, sir, for the opportunity to work on this wonderful house."

Holly hung up and put her phone back in her pocket. Merlin looked up at her and cocked his head. "He wanted to make sure there weren't any hiccups he should know about. I know, I know, he sounds more than a little anxious to get the key he always talks about." She picked up her cat. "Miss Dee wanted to know about it, too. She looked relieved he didn't have it. I think this mysterious key is more important than people want to tell me."

****

When Ray returned to work, Lucas met him at the door. "The town elders want to see you right away."

"Why? I'm not aware of any problems I've caused. Do you know what they want with me?"

Lucas grinned. "Those nosy old men want an update on the Gordon house situation. It's come to their attention you've spent a lot of time with one Holly Stevens. After the whole diner incident, they want more information about her. So, since you've been with her more than a few days, have you fallen for Ms. Stevens? You can tell me anything, you know."

Ray's cheeks flamed. "Cut it out, Lucas. She needs help with the house. It's bigger than she realized. The yard is a huge mess. I want to be nice."

"You better watch it, my friend. Parker and I were nice, and we ended up married."

"Not discussing this with you." Ray grinned as he opened the car door. "I think I'll leave now, boss. I'll be back in a little while."

He drove the two miles to town hall and parked in the side lot near the park. He got out and took a quick walk to see how far the preparations had gone. He smiled. There were a lot more booths and decorations than last year. Mrs. Hall really did go all out this time. Her events were big, but this bordered on grandiose. What made this year special? The one difference in town this year...He stopped. Holly was the difference. She'd certainly had an effect on him.

Could she somehow be responsible for the bigger party? Mrs. Hall didn't even know she would be here now. He walked back to the front of the building. He thought back to the night before her arrival. The house had woken up. He'd seen it; the anticipation in the air surrounded him. At the time, it scared him, but now, it felt, how to describe it? Could the house be happy? The longer Holly remained in it, the happier the house became.

He walked up to the mayor's office, Holly and the house still on his mind. He knocked on the door and entered when called. "You wanted to see me, Mayor Jacobs?"

"Sit down, Burnett." Ray stood near the door as the mayor walked toward him. "There's been a shift in the town's magic. Have you felt it?"

Ray took a step back as the town elders scowled at him. "Yes, sir. I did feel the change in the air. I think Garland Falls is happy Holly is here to fix up the Gordon house. I get a sense this change is right. It will be good for the town and the people."

The mayor stepped closer to him. "You mean, you think this girl will help you fit in better, don't you. She stood up for you the other day at the diner."

"If you mean, did I ask her to, I didn't. I offered to help Holly with the house so she can get what Randolph promised her. If she completes the job within the thirty days, he'll pay her a huge amount of money."

"Dee Warner called me," the mayor said as he walked behind his desk. "She's under the impression Holly Stevens came here for not only the Gordon house, but for you."

"She's mistaken. I do my job and I want to help a friend."

"Friend?" The mayor snorted as he sat with a thump. "My information tells me you want to be more than friends with this girl. Listen to me, Burnett. We allow you to remain in Garland Falls on the word of Dee Warner and Adelaide Hall. We expect more information from you than this miniscule amount you've given us. Now tell me. Has she found the Master Key yet?"

Ray clenched his hands at his side, to hide how much they shook at the mayor's interrogation. "No, sir, not yet. She found the keyring which opens all the doors, but they don't work without the Master Key. I'll let you know when she finds it."

"You had better. I don't want you to keep any information from us." The mayor picked up a pen and flipped open a folder. "And Burnett, when the door to the Dark Lands opens, go through it."

Ray left the mayor's office, his chest tight, his stomach sour. As much as he'd wanted to slam the door, he'd restrained himself. The town elders already disliked and mistrusted him. It wouldn't do to give them another reason to insult him. It shouldn't matter his father sat on the Dark Land hierarchy, second to his uncle, Despair. Why did he have to be blamed for his parentage?

"Ray?" Mrs. Hall said. "What's wrong, dear?"

"I had to meet with the mayor and the town elders. They didn't even suggest it this time. They told me, in no uncertain terms, to go back to the Dark Lands." He glanced at her. "I don't know why they hate me so much. I've never given them any reason to."

"Come to my office. We'll talk more there."

He followed the stout older woman down the hall to her office. She shut the door as he sat on the little couch against the wall. She sat next to him and held his hand. "When you're ready, tell me what's on your mind."

His trembling slowed, then quit. "After Holly finishes the house, she'll go back home to Vermont," he said. "I think I'll leave, too. I can't stay in this town any longer. Every time I go to Main Street, I can feel the animosity toward me grow." He held his head, his voice thick with years of unshed tears. "I can't take it anymore."

"Ray, you can't return to the Dark Lands. Despair has forbidden it. He's spelled out dire consequences for you if you go back."

"I'd still rather be anywhere than here."

"Talk to Lucas. Maybe he and his wife can make those old fools see reason. I'm sure his parents can. They have a lot of clout." She smiled and lifted his chin. "You have more friends here than enemies. Some of those friends can be very persuasive."

"You mean because the Callahans are one of the original families and the mayor respects them."

Mrs. Hall winked. "More like fears them. They have ties to the Green Prince, and you know the prince doesn't like to be bothered. The mayor doesn't want to lose their support. You tell Lucas what the mayor said and believe me, he'll have his parents on those old goats quicker than you can spit."

He gave her a small smile. "Thanks, Mrs. Hall. You always know how to cheer me up."

"I admire you, Ray. You face so much adversity here, but you still smile and are kind to everyone you meet. I'll let Dee Warner know what's happened, too. Trust me. She won't put up with their nonsense any more than I will. You go on back to work." She glanced at the door and narrowed her eyes. "I've got my own work to do here."

Ray walked out to his car and glanced up at the window he knew to be the mayor's office. He felt a little sorry for the mayor and the town elders when Mrs. Hall got to their office. The stout little lady would be on her way there right now to read them the riot act. He didn't know how he'd gotten so lucky to have such a powerful woman on his side.

Chapter Fifteen

Holly grabbed Ray's hand and dragged him inside when he arrived. "You've got to see this. Come on."

Ray dodged Merlin as the cat ran up the stairs ahead of them. "Slow down, Holly. We might trip, and I don't want to explain how you got another injury to Sean at the hospital. What's happened now?"

They reached the third floor and Holly walked him down to the end of the hall. "I heard a noise up here earlier. I came up and I saw this door. It's the same door from my dream, but now it looks different."

Ray stared at the door and frowned. "Okay, how is it different? It's a plain wood door."

Holly looked at him and then the door. "You can't see the key carved in it? The door is white and has all kinds of colors running through it. Are you sure you can't see it?" He shook his head. Holly grabbed his hand and laid it against the wood. "Can you feel the carving?"

Ray blinked several times and narrowed his eyes. "I can see it now. I can see the key and the colors." He pulled his hand away from hers and the door faded back to normal. He held her hand again and the door appeared as she saw it. "I think this door is meant for you. I can see what you see when I hold your hand."

"Maybe it means it's meant for both of us." She looked down at the cat. "Merlin can see it, too."

"Cats often see what people can't. Maybe when you find the Master Key, it will open this door. Come on. You need to get back to cleaning and I want to make more progress on the yard." As they walked downstairs, Ray held up her bandaged hand. "How's the wound?"

"I changed the bandage earlier today and it's almost healed. I don't know what Dr. O'Brien put on it, but it's already closed up and hasn't given me any problems. It should be healed by tomorrow."

"I knew Sean's salve would do the trick."

Holly pulled up music on her phone and she started on the library while Ray went back out to the gardens. After an hour, Holly dropped her sponge in the bucket and arched her back. She walked outside and twisted and stretched. She bent over to lay her hands flat against the porch. She paused when she saw Ray watching her.

"The mattress on the bed isn't great," she said. "Between it and work, my back is killing me. I have to tell Mr. Gordon to replace it, even though it looks brand new."

"Here, let me help." He walked over and wrapped her arms around her chest and lifted her off her feet. He gave her a quick jerk, he set her back down. "Better?"

She twisted from side to side. "Oh yeah. It hasn't felt this good in ages. Thanks. Okay, back to work. I still have to finish the two more rooms on the ground floor, then start on the upper floors. You have no idea what the backyard looks like yet. I'm pretty sure the fence needs to be sanded and repainted, too."

"I'll ask Lucas if he and his brother can help with some of the yard work." He pulled his gloves back on and picked up the rake. "Those two can pick out what plant or flower will look best around the property." He grinned. "They may even help with the fence. They'll know what the yard will need to complement the house."

"Are you sure they won't mind?" When he nodded, she smiled. "Awesome. Soon I'll have the army Mr. Gordon should've hired to begin with." She raised her arms over her head in a triumphant salute. "To work, my friend."

Holly walked back inside while Ray got back to work in the upper tier garden. When they stopped, the library sparkled as the sunlight faded and the first garden looked much improved. He knocked on the door before he walked in. Merlin followed him and inspected every corner and the furniture. He sat in the middle of the rug and stared at them.

"I think he likes what you've accomplished so far," Ray said.

Holly bent down and scratched Merlin under his chin. "Thank you for your approval on my work. We'll have to let you look at the yard when it's finished." He meowed and laid his paw on her hand. "You're the best, buddy. I'll make sure to get you a special treat from Main Street."

When a knock echoed through the house, Holly looked at Ray who smiled. She opened the door and a teenager stood there and held out a pizza box. "I didn't order a pizza."

"Someone did because Mr. Bergetole said to bring it at eight and it's already been paid for."

Ray walked over and gave the teen a ten. "Thanks for the quick delivery, and thank Mr. Bergetole for me again."

The teen nodded and hurried down to his scooter and left as soon as he jumped on it. They shut the door and Holly led the way to the kitchen. She set out paper plates and grabbed two sodas from her small cooler and set the roll of paper towels between them.

"You didn't have to do this you know."

"I know." He opened the box and put one slice on each plate. "I wanted to spend some time with you away from Main Street. I guess you can tell I don't go there very often."

She handed him a paper towel. "I did pick up on the tension when we're there. I'm glad we decided to eat here tonight. It's hard to talk with all the diner noise sometimes. So, what's the story of Ray Burnett? Don't sugar coat any part of your life. I want to know all about you. Like why some people have such a problem with you and some people don't."

"I don't think I can tell you what you want to know." He popped the top of the soda can and listened to the fizz as he watched the tiny bubbles float out. "I'm not sure you would believe me."

She sat back and took a sip of her drink. "I don't know. I might. Miss Dee told me there's powerful magic around me and I'm not sure how to process her information. I can see a white door upstairs and you can see it when you hold my hand. A purple door under the stairs is weird, and keys fall on the floor when they shouldn't. I've also had strange visions, talked to a ghost, and visited Mrs. Santa Claus. So, tell me what you can, and I promise I'll believe you."

"Okay." He took a deep breath, then blurted out, "I'm not human." He paused to watch her for any sign of disbelief before he continued. "I'm from the Dark Lands where the more, not evil, but not entirely good fairies live. My father is Strife, and my uncle is Despair. My uncle tried to destroy a magical rose last year. Since my father's family is from the Dark Lands, people expect me to follow his path."

Holly stared at him, then nodded. "Not quite what I expected but, hey, we all have black sheep in our families somewhere. It explains why people would treat you the way they do. What about your mother? Where is she from?"

"She's from the Light Side. She works with Nature and is part of her court. My mother looks after newborn animals until they're old enough to go to their destined homes."

"It must be why Merlin likes you so much." The object of her observation jumped into Ray's lap and curled up. "See? He must sense your connection to animals."

"Sometimes I wish I could leave Garland Falls, but it isn't possible. Despair has forbidden me to return to the Dark Lands and the Light Siders don't want me there either. I'm lucky Lucas and his family accept me. I wish the rest of this town would, too."

"They will; I'll make sure of it." She reached across the table and squeezed his hand. "Don't let their opinions bother you. You have Dr. O'Brien, Lucas, Miss Dee, Sally, and a whole bunch of other people who like you for who you are. I liked you from the moment I met you." She let his hand go to give him another slice of pizza. "Of course, Merlin thought you were beyond handsome. He told me so in no uncertain terms."

Ray scratched the cat behind his ears and smiled when Merlin purred. "So, you didn't think so, too? I thought you were beautiful."

She smiled. "He thought you were handsome. I thought you were beyond gorgeous."

"Do you want to try to inflate my ego, Ms. Stevens?"

"I want to build your self-esteem up, Mr. Burnett." She wiped her mouth. "I do have an ulterior motive. I don't want to lose your help. I find if I pay you in compliments, that works the best."

He toasted her comment with his soda can. "Thanks, but I would help you anyway. Here's to the house starting to sparkle like the old days." They tapped the cans together. "We'd better get back to work. I can help you in here since it's gotten dark out."

"I'll take all the help I can get."

They went back to the library. Holly wiped down the books, and Ray took care of cleaning the ceiling lights. She opened the desk drawers to look under papers and assorted supplies. "I don't think I'll ever find the key Mr. Gordon wants. He got excited when I told him about the keyring in the rolltop desk. I examined every inch of the desk and the keyring turned out to be the only keys there. I guess the missing key opens a secret door or a safe."

"Let's finish up and we'll talk some more," he said.

They put the cleaning supplies away and Holly took a deep breath of the fresh summer air. Once again, she knew she'd made the right decision to open the windows first. She led him back to the living room and turned the volume down on her phone but kept the smooth jazz music on. They sat on the couch, and she turned to him.

"What do you want to talk about? Do you know why Mr. Gordon is so anxious to get the antique key?"

Ray nodded. "The key he wants is the Master Key to this house. The other keys won't work until the Master Key is joined with them."

"And what does the Master Key do?"

He took a deep breath. "The Master Key will only work for the true owner of this house. Each one of those doors you found is a doorway to another place in the fairy realms. The door with the rose on it opens into a safe room. Evil can't go in there, no matter how much it wants to. Lucas has the same door in his office at the nursery."

"So, the green door in the kitchen leads to…"

"The North Pole," Ray said. "This house was built on a nexus point. It's the central gateway to the different realms. It's why the house is so important to the town. Without it, all the portals would be in danger."

"Well, I'm happy to know I'm not crazy. What you said makes a certain kind of sense. I understand now why everyone wants the Master Key." She leaned against the couch, closed her eyes, and rubbed her temples. She was quiet for a few minutes, then sat straight up. "Did you feel a weird shift in the air?"

"Maybe. What did you feel?"

"The house feels…happy." She took his hand and stood, glancing around the room. "It sounds like it breathed a sigh of relief. It feels like tension has left here."

Ray moved closer to her. "It does feel different in here now. I think it waited for you to learn the truth about what this house is. I think you're more important to Garland Falls and the Gordon house than you know."

"Ray, I'm a glorified maid. Yes, I discovered some strange things here and this place likes me, but this isn't my house. It belongs to Randolph Gordon and his daughter."

"Henrietta always said the house would know when the rightful heir would come. I don't think it's Randolph Gordon or his daughter." He took her hands. "I'm pretty sure you're the rightful heir to the Darkling Street house. You're the Keeper of the Keys."

Chapter Sixteen

"You're telling me this now, too? I'm sorry, but I have to disagree with all of you." Holly rubbed her forehead and paced. "I'm not related to the Gordons. I can't be the rightful heir to this humongous house. I'd never even heard of Garland Falls until I got hired. There's nothing special about me so I can't be the new Keeper."

He pulled her down to sit on the couch. "I'm sure everyone is right, including me. It's why you can see the rainbows in the white door upstairs. It's why you can feel and see the odd occurrences here and I can't. I believe you can hear the house speak to you. It wouldn't talk to just anyone, but it would to the one who rightfully belongs here."

"Wow. First, I find out you're not even human and you have some dark lineage so people don't like you. Then, you tell me about a Master Key which opens doors to different dimensions. You told me this house is a nexus point. This is a lot of information to digest. You really agree with Henrietta's ghost and Miss Dee that this house is mine?" She drummed her fingers on her legs for a few minutes while he watched her, not saying a word. "I did have a weird déjà vu sense when I first got here. Garland Falls felt familiar to me. Maybe I do belong in this house after all."

"I know it's a lot to take in all at once." Ray pulled

her into his arms and held her close as they sat on the couch again. "We'll go back and see Miss Dee again. Maybe she can get Mrs. Hall to come by and talk to you, too. Like you tell me all the time, you aren't alone in this. You have friends who can help you."

She laid her arm across his stomach and held him tight. "I know. I think I need a little time to get used to all this." Her eyes drifted closed as she yawned. "Good night, Ray. I don't know what I'd do without you."

"Good night, Holly."

He laid his cheek on top of her head and let himself drift away.

****

"Lucas, can I talk to you for a minute?" Ray said the next morning when he got to work.

Lucas looked up from where he re-potted petunias. "Sure, Ray. You know I can always spare you some time."

"Did you feel the magic shift last night?"

"Yep. The whole town felt it. I know because my mother called me, and she was the first of many." Lucas grinned. "I think you'll be able to tell me why it happened."

Ray lifted a new bag of potting soil onto the table and tore it open and helped with the petunias. "I told Holly about the Master Key. I'm pretty sure she's the new Keeper of the Keys."

They worked in silence for a few minutes before Lucas spoke. "How did you come to this conclusion? What did she say? Has new information come to light?"

"She found a door on the third floor. She claimed she saw rainbow colors in the white paint. I couldn't see them until she held my hand. After I told her about

120

the keys, the house settled, like it blew out a breath. The tension is gone from the place and the atmosphere is lighter, like people say it used to be. When I left there this morning, I came right here to talk to you."

"Hold it," Lucas said as he held his hands up. "You spent the night there with her?"

Ray cheeks heated. "Well, yes, but it's not what you think. We were on the couch. I held her when she became upset, and she fell asleep in my arms. So, I stayed."

Lucas laughed. "Raymond, I swear you are headed straight to the altar with this girl. She's made for you, and I've never seen you turn this red before."

"There's a chance you might be right." They turned back to potting the flowers. "I feel at home when we're together. The townspeople's attitudes toward me don't matter when I'm with her."

"Then, my friend, she's the one for you."

He handed Lucas the pots he'd finished. "Do you think you and Parker can help us with the yard? It needs a lot of work, and the iron fence needs to be sanded and repainted."

He nodded. "I'm sure we can squeeze in a couple of days to give you two a hand. The wife is out of town again on another assignment for the Holiday Security Agency, so I've got extra time."

"How long will she be away?"

"Only a week. She's got a short assignment for a change. I think I saw more of her before we were married than I do now."

They walked back into the shop and put the new flowers on an empty shelf. "I tell you what," Ray said. "Get more jelly beans and she won't be able to resist staying home."

The two laughed as they opened the store and got ready for the morning customers.

****

"I'm glad you let me come see you so early, Miss Dee. I hope I didn't wake you. Ray said you could help me make sense of what he told me last night."

"Pish tosh, my dear. I'm always up early." Dee handed her a cup of tea and placed a cinnamon roll on a plate in front of her. "I'll be happy to help in any way I can. Now, what do you need to know?"

"Well, he also said Mrs. Hall might be able to help, too."

Dee sipped her tea. "If Adelaide needs to be brought in, I'll call her. Now tell me what he told you."

Holly related what Ray had said the previous night. As she recounted the information, she still couldn't believe half of what she told Dee. "I can't be the rightful heir to the house. I didn't even know the Gordons until Randolph called me."

Dee sat quietly while she studied Holly. "How do you feel about Garland Falls and the house on Darkling Street? Tell me what appeals to you."

"When I first arrived, I found the town to be a lot bigger than I thought, but still small enough to be quaint and adorable. Main Street is incredible, and the people are so nice to me. I hate the fact they treat Ray like he's some kind of pariah. I fell in love with the house as soon as I saw it, but it intimidated me. I mean, the place is huge and I still have two floors to clean in two weeks." Holly sipped her tea. "And that doesn't include the attic, but I haven't found a basement, so I hope there isn't one. If Ray hadn't helped me, I wouldn't even be done with the ground floor."

"Did your feelings about Ray change when he told you about his origin?"

Holly stared at Dee. "No way. My feelings for him could never change. I like Ray." She stared at her teacup. "A lot. He's so nice and generous and my cat loves him. I think his big flaw is he cares too much about what people think about him. It felt wrong to disbelieve him. I know he told me the truth."

"What about you? You say you like him a lot. Do you feel more for him than you want to admit?"

She thought about Dee's question. Had she started to love Ray? She'd known him for two weeks, but time shouldn't make a difference, should it? She'd never had such strong emotions about anyone before, ever. Her past boyfriends didn't deserve the title. They would go on a couple of dates and that would be it.

"I think I do love him, Miss Dee. We spend a lot of time together, you know, working on the house. Whenever people treat him badly, I want, no, I need to defend him. When he left this morning, I swear the house felt happy he stayed with me."

"He spent the night with you?"

Holly stared at her napkin to hide her burning cheeks. "It's not what you think. I kind of fell asleep on him while we sat on the couch. I think between all the work we did and what he said, it wiped me out."

"Perfectly understandable." Dee picked up the cups and took them to the kitchen. When she came back, she sat next to Holly. "I do believe I'll call Adelaide. She likes to be kept in the loop on these types of matters. Don't you worry about Ray. He has a lot of allies here and now he has you, too. You'll help him find his voice to stand up against those who dislike him."

Holly picked at the tablecloth while Dee went to call her friend. She knew she should leave this strange little town and forget the promised money. As soon as she thought about when she would leave, her stomach soured and bile burned her throat. Garland Falls wanted her to stay, and she wanted to stay more than ever. Randolph Gordon could be considered the one hiccup in her future. He wanted the house prepped for his daughter and he sure wouldn't give the manor to her. What he would ask for it would be way out of her price range.

She fell in love with the house the minute she saw it. The more she cleaned it, the more she knew she and the house belonged together. The size of the place no longer intimidated her. She fantasized about large parties in the house and how the yard would look at Christmas with lights and decorations everywhere. With the preparations for a big Founders Day celebration, the house would've looked great all decked out in a rainbow of colors. The gardens would look spectacular when Ray finished with them.

"Stop it," she whispered. "The house isn't and will never be yours. Get your head out of the clouds and back down here. Your world is to clean homes and battle dust bunnies."

Dee walked back into the dining room and sat. "Adelaide will be here in a few minutes. She had already decided to come here to talk to me. She said she wanted to call me right before I called her." She looked at Holly and smiled. "We both felt a shift in the town last night."

"You mean like an earthquake?"

Dee patted her hand. "More like a magical tremor. I believe it happened when you accepted what Ray told you."

They turned as the front door opened and a stout, older woman walked in. She shed a large straw hat while she dropped her purse on the table. She leaned close to Holly and stared at her.

"So, this is the little lady everyone in town talks about." She grasped Holly's hand and shook it. "We haven't met yet, but I know you. I'm Adelaide Hall. I'd heard how you put the mayor in his place the other day. I must say, I got a good laugh when I pictured his face."

"Holly Stevens. And the mayor deserved every word I said." She shook Mrs. Hall's hand. "It's a pleasure to meet you, Mrs. Hall. Ray speaks very highly of you. I had begun to wonder if I'd ever meet you."

Mrs. Hall chuckled. "You wouldn't have been able to avoid me, my dear. I'm what's known as a fixture in this town."

"Holly, tell Adelaide what you've told me."

Holly cleared her throat. "Well, when I arrived in Garland Falls, the town felt kind of familiar, like I'd been here before. After I started on the house, weird things began to happen. I had a dream where I met Henrietta Gordon's ghost. She told me I'm the rightful heir to her home. The other day while I refilled my steam vac tank, I kind of had a vision. I went through the green door in the kitchen and met Felicity Claus."

She took a deep breath, then continued. "The latest is I found a white door on the third floor with iridescent colors no one can see but me and my cat. Ray could see it when I held his hand. He said I'm the Keeper of the Keys, whatever that means. Last night, he agreed with

Henrietta I'm the rightful heir to the house on Darkling Street. I don't see how it's possible, but after he told me, the house, I don't know, settled or breathed a sigh of relief."

"Yes, yes, yes, we all felt it." Mrs. Hall turned to Dee. "Do you think Randolph Gordon sent her here for reason? After all, he could've sent anyone, and he could have hired more than a single woman to clean his sister's monster of a house."

"When it comes to Garland Falls, anything is possible," Dee said.

Holly held her hands up. "Wait a minute. Henrietta told me she went to her brother and sort of nudged him to hire me. Even though he wants his daughter to have the house, I think Henrietta wants me to take possession of her home."

Mrs. Hall laid her hand on Holly's shoulder. "I'll get in touch with Randolph and find out when he wants his daughter here. I'll tell him about his sister's wishes. You go on back to Darkling Street and leave all this to us. We should know what his plans are by the end of the week."

"Thanks. I should get back to work." She slung her purse over her shoulder. "With all the strange stuff I've learned, I think I've handled it all pretty well." She grinned. "I mean, I haven't run screaming into the night yet, so it's a good sign."

Dee gave her shoulder a gentle pat. "The Darkling Street house is waking up the magic inside you. You may discover you have ties to this little town and not know it yet."

"I'm still not sure about this magic you claim I have, but I guess it's possible."

Holly walked out to her car and knew the two women stared at her. As she drove back toward Darkling Street, she decided to stop on Main Street and look at some of the stores. After all, she did promise Merlin a special treat because he'd been such a good boy. She picked up a can of white albacore tuna and another bag of treats from Mac's general store, some cookies from Heavenly Bites, and a few groceries from the small grocery store nestled in between two other specialty shops.

She walked up to the front door and put the bags down to unlock the door. When no silver cat streak jumped into her arms, she frowned. She set the bags on the floor in the hall and shut the door. An icy chill ran up her spine as her cat appeared to have vanished. He always greeted her when she came home.

"Merlin? Where are you, buddy?" She shook the bag of treats. "I got you a surprise."

Her throat tightened as she checked all the downstairs rooms. As she walked by the purple door under the stairs, she stared. It opened a crack and darkness appeared to leak out. Cold tremors gripped her as she pulled the door open, and a loud gasp escaped her before she could stop it.

The door didn't open to any room. It opened to a whole other world. Gnarled trees with black bark and drooping branches swayed over brown grass. Bushes were choked out by the undergrowth around them, but her breath caught when she looked up. Angry gray clouds covered a weak red sun in a dark purple sky. If she had any doubts about what Ray said about the doors opening to other worlds, they were immediately dispelled.

A little man with a red cap on his head jumped out of the bushes and brandished a large stick. "What do you want?" he demanded.

She couldn't decide if the threatening tone in his voice, his piercing black eyes, or the large stick he held scared her the most. "The door opened a little. I thought my cat came in here. Have you seen him? He's large with long, silver-gray fur."

The little man bared sharp teeth. "If such a critter came through here, he would've been my lunch." He narrowed his eyes as he glared at her. "You are the new Keeper of the Keys. Don't come here again until the Master Key is in your possession. Until then, stay on your own side of the door." He yanked on the door and slammed it closed.

Holly leaned against the wall as tremors gripped her and wouldn't let her go. How did the door open? She certainly hadn't had a vision this time. Did the man live in that world or in her closet? The colors in this world weirded her out, but more importantly, where could Merlin have gone? How did the man with the red hat know people called her the Keeper of the Keys? Times like this, she was tempted to get in her car and drive away from Garland Falls. If it weren't for Ray, she would've been gone by now.

"Merlin," she yelled again. "Come here, buddy. I'm kind of freaked out right about now and I could use some kitty hugs."

A silver streak tore down the steps and jumped into her arms. His claws dug into her shoulder through her shirt, but she didn't pry him loose. She cried as she held him close and didn't care that it made his fur stick to her face. They both turned to stare at the purple door.

"I'm so glad you're safe. That door needs to be blocked right now." She got to the other side of a heavy, oak storage cabinet near the kitchen. She shoved it down the hall and jammed it next to the door. "If this doesn't hold it, nothing will."

She picked up Merlin and sat on the couch in the newly cleaned living room. "I think we both need a minute. You know, when I go out, I might have to take you with me from now on. I didn't like the little man in there. He said he would eat you." She rubbed his head and smiled as his purr rumbled against her chest. "I can't let you be some weird guy's dinner. I wish I knew how the door opened up. It had been locked tight. This is the first door that opened when I wasn't asleep or having a weird vision. I bet this is an important development."

She continued to pet Merlin and stared off into space. The appearance of the Dark Land behind the door proved this house was indeed a nexus point for different realms. If she hadn't been so scared of the little man, she would've yelled right back at him. It was one thing to be told different worlds existed, quite another to see one with her own eyes.

Merlin meowed and headbutted her collarbone. She buried her face in his fur again. She had her furry buddy safe in her arms and he gave her all the reassurance she needed. With her companion beside her, she would finish cleaning the house and tell Randolph she belonged here more than he did.

Chapter Seventeen

Holly gave Ray two sandwiches and double handfuls of chips for lunch. Thank goodness she remembered to bring her tiny refrigerator with her. She cleared her throat and drew circles on the water ring on the table. "There was an incident today and I don't want you to freak out."

He set his soda down and stared at her. "I don't think it's a promise I can keep, but go ahead. What happened?"

"When I got home today, the purple door under the stairs had opened by itself. I saw this strange little man wearing a red cap. He called me the Keeper of the Keys and not to open the door until I had the Master Key. He also said he would eat Merlin. I pushed the oak cabinet in front of the door so it won't open again."

Ray squeezed his lips together for a solid minute before he spoke. "Okay. I won't freak out, but this isn't good. The door shouldn't have been able to open without the key. As far as I know, no one in the Dark Lands has a key to this particular door."

"But why would he want to eat my cat?"

"I'm sure he wanted to scare you." He winked at her and smiled a little. "Most people in the Dark Lands don't eat animals like cats."

Holly set her sandwich down. "Wait a second. Did you say *most* people don't eat cats? I hate when I have

130

to leave Merlin alone in this house all the time. Should I take him with me when I go out?"

"Trust me. He'll be fine." Ray smiled when Merlin jumped up on a chair and put his front paws on the table. He scratched him behind the ears. "Merlin will be okay by himself since you blocked the door. Where did you get this amazing boy anyway?"

"He kind of found me," she said. "I came home from work one day and this poor bedraggled kitten found his way to my porch. He had matted fur and a bad eye infection in both eyes. I cleaned him up and took him to the vet to make sure he hadn't been injured. The vet proclaimed him healthy. I put up flyers and asked around but no one knew where he came from, so I kept him. I called him Merlin because he appeared like magic."

"A very appropriate name. He's a wonderful companion for you." He gazed at her. "I'm sure he's meant to be yours."

"After all I've learned in the past week, I wouldn't be surprised." She rubbed the cat's head. "He's been my buddy for three years now."

"I believe you two will be together for a long time."

She smiled at Ray. "I hope you're right. I love this guy."

They finished their dinner and Holly walked Ray to the front door. "I should finish the downstairs today. There's not much more to do. There's a sunroom at the back of the house near the laundry room. I can tackle it tomorrow while you're at work. Maybe the key will turn up when I start on the second floor. How's the yard look? After this weekend, I'll be halfway through my time."

"Not bad. It will take a lot of work. When Lucas and his brother come to help, I'm sure it will go quicker." He opened the front door and paused. "What does Miss Dee say about the key?"

"She called it the Master Key, too. She wants me to tell her before I tell Randolph when I find it. It's weird how so many people want it."

"Since it's the Master Key to make all the others work, it doesn't surprise me." He gave her a brief hug. "We'll figure it out. Any more trouble with the mean-spirited plantstand?"

"Nope. I put it back in the place where I found it and have had no issues. I think it learned its lesson." She pointed to herself. "Don't mess with this lady's cleaning service."

He chuckled. "I think that's a good lesson to learn. See you tonight."

After he left, Holly went down to the sunroom. "At least this room isn't too bad," she said to Merlin, who meowed in agreement. "Let's get started. I'd like to get this last room done."

She grabbed her stepstool and started with the cobwebs in the ceiling corners and wiped off the dust. The concrete floor could be scrubbed with little effort. She pulled the cushions off the two chairs and took them outside. The air became thick with dust as she beat them with a broom. She went back inside and opened the windows. Fresh air flowed in and cleaned out the last of the mustiness.

She left the cushions out in the sunshine and turned her attention to the small, glass-topped table. She grabbed her bucket and scrubbed the dust and grime off until it gleamed in the afternoon light. The curtains waved in the breeze and covered Holly before they slid off her shoulders in a gentle caress.

She smiled. "You're welcome, house. Before you know it, you'll be beautiful again." She sighed as she picked up the bucket. "I hope Mr. Gordon's daughter appreciates you as much as I do. I wish I could stay here."

The breeze stilled and melancholy filled Holly as she thought of someone other than herself in the house. The more she worked on the manor, the more she loved it. Sure, it creeped her out when she first arrived, but that feeling had long passed. The oddness she'd come to associate with the manor had become more familiar to her than her own apartment. She didn't even notice the strangeness any longer. The Darkling Street manor wanted her here and no one else.

"I'm glad you're haunted by Henrietta or I would've been out of here before I even started the work on you. Ray's a big help, too." The curtains fluttered again. "I'm glad you like him. He's great, isn't he?" She shook her head as she went to empty the bucket. "Good grief. I've talked to the house like it understands me."

The house shuddered and threw her off balance for a moment. Merlin walked up and cocked his head as he stared at her. She had to laugh at the absurdity. Somehow, she'd insulted the house and Merlin sat in front of her to give her a disappointed look.

"Fine. I'm sorry. If I'd known you listened to me, I never would've said it." She continued down to the laundry room to pour out the bucket. "You know, I often talk to the houses I clean. I'm not sure if it's for my benefit or theirs, but it makes me feel a little less lonely when I do. After all, I'm my whole company. Not a lot of people to have a conversation with, you know?"

She traded the bucket for the heavy-duty bathroom cleaners and headed to the stairs to start on the upstairs bathrooms. "I don't know why they needed bathrooms on every floor, but I guess if a big family lived here, it would be a good idea."

She stopped short in the hallway. A clear picture filled her vision of children as they ran through the halls, and their laughter filled the house. The vision pulled back and she saw herself as she stood arm in arm with Ray. Did the vision mean they would be married and would live here? They were expected to have, it looked like, five children? She shook her head and rubbed her eyes. The house came back into focus in its present state.

"What happened?" She stared at the walls and grabbed her rag to wipe them down. "Do you mean to tell me I'm supposed to live here with Ray and we'll have a whole passel of kids?" Warmth surrounded her and made her smile. "Oh, house, if it could be true, I'd be the happiest woman in the world."

A knock on the front door made her jump and Holly peeled off her rubber gloves. She stared at her palm, still amazed how fast the cut had healed. She opened the door and Mrs. Hall and Miss Dee stood there.

"Hi. I didn't expect to see you ladies so soon." She opened the door wider and let them come in. "Can I offer you some lemonade or tea?"

"No, thank you, dear," Mrs. Hall said. She turned

to her friend. "Can you feel the difference here, Dee?"

Dee nodded. "The house had such a dark, bleak feel to it after Henrietta passed away." She turned to Holly. "Ever since you came, we've all felt a change around the town." She walked over and laid a hand on the wall. "This house is happy you've come. Adelaide and I believe it waited for you."

"I feel the same way, too," Holly said. "Can I tell you about a strange vision I had a moment ago? I saw me and Ray in this house with a whole bunch of kids. What do you think?"

Mrs. Hall nodded. "It's what I've felt. This house needs you and no other, except maybe Ray. Well, we won't keep you. We needed to check out the magic we've sensed flowing over the town. It originates from here. Even Garland Falls has a more cheerful feel to it since you've come. The magic waited for someone. We're so happy it's you."

Holly twisted the rubber gloves in her hands. "But I won't stay when my work is done. Mr. Gordon's daughter is supposed to take over after I've finished. I don't think he'll let me buy it."

"Don't worry about the future," Dee said. "All will work out the way it's supposed to. We came by for a quick look and to confirm what we suspected. You and Ray come see me again soon, Holly. I'm sure we'll have lots more to talk about when you do."

"Of course. Goodbye, ladies. Stop by any time."

After Holly shut the door, she turned to Merlin who stared at her. "Okay. The ladies' impromptu visit felt weird, right? I mean, they didn't stay very long. I don't think I'll ever get used to this." When he rubbed her ankles, she knew he agreed. "I guess all we can do now is get back to work. All I have left is to wash the walls and then I believe the downstairs will be done."

Her phone buzzed in her pocket. "Hello, Mr. Gordon. Yes, all is on schedule, and I should be done on time. I wanted to tell you the new kitchen appliances will be here this weekend. I'm glad you let me update them." She smiled at Merlin while she listened. "Yes, I'll take care of all of it. The chimney crew will be here on Monday. No, I haven't found the key yet, but I'll look for it everywhere. Goodbye, sir."

She stuffed the phone back in her pants pocket. "Let's get to work, buddy. You know, if luck is with us, we might get this place done on time."

Chapter Eighteen

Holly finished the first room on the second floor, when the rumble of a lawn mower reached her. Warmth spread through her knowing Ray worked right outside. With all she learned from Miss Dee and Mrs. Hall, she knew he wouldn't laugh at her if she told him she talked to the house and it kind of answered.

She put away her supplies and went to the living room windows. She loved to watch him as he mowed the yard in neat rows. He walked one way, then turned and headed back the other way. He had a hypnotic grace to his movements and the vision came back to her. Yes, she could now see herself and Ray with a bunch of kids. Would he see it too, or would he run for the hills? She shook her head. No. He wouldn't run from a future with promised happiness.

"I'm glad you accepted the future I see for you," Henrietta's ghost said. "I've known all along Ray deserved someone special."

Holly blinked and she stood in Henrietta's bedroom again. "How did I get here?"

"I needed you here." The ghost floated by the window, also interested in watching Ray work. "You were born to be here. You hold the magic this house, and Garland Falls in particular, needs."

Holly walked over to stand by the ghost. "You know Randolph won't let me have this place. I'm nobody to him."

Henrietta smiled at her. "But you're somebody to me. I love the way you talk to the house. It's happy you're here to take care of it."

"I think I hurt its feelings a little, but we made up," Holly said. She chuckled. "I always talk to the houses I work on. I can almost feel them be happy when someone acknowledges them."

"Houses are more alive than people realize." Henrietta gazed at her bedroom. "I loved this old place when I lived. Randolph didn't share my views and left as soon as he could. We had our last big fight when he said he wanted to tear this place down."

"I don't think he could," Holly said. She followed the ghost as she floated around the room. "Your house has a solidity to it. Maybe it's why he wants his daughter here. If she's as nasty as you say, her negativity could poison the house so it would want to be torn down."

Henrietta gave the impression she rubbed her chin. "I'd never considered that possibility. Lydia would hurt the house, whereas you have helped it. I can feel the magic grow in strength the longer you work here." She turned to Holly and smiled. "You've given my home the life it has missed for far too many years."

"I'll do all I can to give the house back its glory. Ray has been a huge help with the yard and some of the inside work. Your house always feels happier when he's here." She walked back to the window and watched him work for a few more minutes. "I'm afraid of Lydia and I'm not sure why. I've never met her, so I don't know what kind of person she is. I'm not one to judge based on others' opinions."

"I know. You have a kind heart, Holly Stevens, but also a strong spirit. You'll know what to do when the time comes."

"Henrietta, where is the Master Key? So many people are concerned about its location and are happy your brother doesn't have it yet. Can you give me any clue to where it might be?"

The ghost shook her head. "I wish I could, but I'm blocked by a force to tell you how to find it. This is one question you'll have to answer on your own." Henrietta's form began to fade. "I'll try to talk to you again soon, and don't worry about Merlin. I'll make sure he stays safe."

"Thank you. I do worry about him."

Holly blinked and she stood back in front of the living room window. Henrietta said the house had gotten stronger. If the magic here had increased, could it be the reason the purple door opened on its own? If true, why didn't the other doors also open on their own? Why couldn't one of the nice doors open? Wonderful. Now she had even more questions to add to the ones she didn't have answered.

"I really wish I knew how she keeps summoning me to her room," she muttered.

Ray had shut off the mower and wiped his forehead. He waved and she smiled and waved back. She took a deep breath and blew it out. Whether she liked it or not, she would have to get used to these visions or blackouts where she talked to ghosts. She looked around the living room, pleased by how much better it looked.

"You know what, house? I think we'll have a fun relationship the whole time I'm here."

The curtains fluttered against her arm, and she laughed, before they settled back down.

****

As Ray cut the high grass, he knew Holly watched him. Her gaze warmed him more than the summer sun. He'd glanced up at her at one point and thought she looked odd. Her arms hung straight down at her sides and she'd lost the smile she'd had.

He'd looked up at that point and saw a soft, white glow emanate from the same third floor window. He knew now the window opened into Henrietta's bedroom. Had the woman's ghost made another appearance? Had she decided to speak to Holly again? Until Holly had come to Garland Falls, the house had remained still and silent for seven long years. Now, its former owner had returned at the same time Holly had arrived.

He shook his head and smiled. Coincidences were laughed at in Garland Falls. Every occurrence in his town happened for a reason. The one reason he could think of was the town and the house wanted Holly here. From what she said, the house wanted him here, too. Heck with the mayor and all of his prejudice. Better people than him wanted Ray and this very important residence wanted him, too.

Yardwork filled him with peace and a warmth he felt in only Holly's presence. "You want me to stay here with her, don't you?" he murmured. The tall grass brushed against his legs with a feather light touch. "You know I want to be here. I've watched you for years and I've seen how the town fears you. We have that in common, don't we?" He gazed up at the house. "If we're together, maybe we can change some perceptions of both of us. Maybe Holly is the one to make it happen."

He finished the front yard, and the thick grass had been hard to get through. He wiped sweat from his forehead and walked up to the front door. Before he knocked, she threw the door open and hugged him tight.

"Hey, I don't know what brought this on, but I'll take it every time," he said. "What else happened? I know because I saw you and you looked strange for a minute."

"I watched you cut the grass and had another vision or whatever it is. Henrietta's ghost talked to me again. She is so happy you're here with me." She looked up at him. "I'm happy you're here, too."

"Nice to know I'm appreciated by someone." He shut the door and they walked to the kitchen. He grabbed a glass while he turned on the water and let it run for a few minutes to get cold. "What else did she say?"

"We think Randolph wants his daughter here so she can poison the house. Then, he should be able to tear it down."

Ray sat at the table and considered her words. "I have to say, I never thought about the possibility he'd want to destroy the house. You know now it's the portal to different realms. If the house is torn down, all the gateways could go haywire."

She nodded. "And I can't let him know my suspicions." Holly walked over to the doorway and ran her hand down the dark wood frame. "I want this house, but I don't think it's possible. The house and I have talked a few times now."

He smiled. "And what did the house say?"

She grinned when Merlin jumped in his lap and stared at him. "The house doesn't talk, silly, I talk to it. There are times though, I can feel what it wants from me." She paused and looked away. "It gave me a vision of the two of us and we lived here with our children."

Ray choked and coughed for several minutes. "What?"

She shrugged. "It's true. This house wants us to be together."

"What do you want?" Did he want to know her answer? If she said she didn't want the future shown to her, he'd be devastated. If she said she wanted him in her life, he'd fly to the moon and back. "I mean, visions aren't always accurate."

She took his hand. "I think this one is. Every time I think of my life without you in it, I get not just sad, but really depressed. When I think about when I have to leave, I get almost physically sick. The house wants me to stay, and it wants me to stay with you." She laid her hand against the wall and smiled at him. "I think we both need you."

He barely restrained himself from jumping up and down at her words. She wanted him. He wouldn't ask for another thing in his life. His chair wobbled and almost threw him on the floor. Okay, he could take a hint. The house wanted him, too. And Holly's explanation made sense now. The house had its own personality.

"I want you in my life, too. I believe you're what's been missing." A quick wiggle of his chair made him add, "Yes, house, you've been missing from my life also."

"So, now what do we do?" she asked. "We still have to find the Master Key. I promised Miss Dee I'd let her know I found it before I tell Mr. Gordon."

"The mayor and the town elders also want to know when we find it." Ray gazed at her. "I don't think we should tell anyone when we find it."

"Except for Miss Dee. I think she's the one we can trust with information this important."

"You're right. We tell Miss Dee and no one else." He drank the rest of his water. "Did Henrietta tell you where it might be hidden?"

Holly shook her head. "She said a force prevents her from telling me where it is. We'll have to search the old-fashioned way."

"All right. The old-fashioned way it is." He stood and pulled her up with him. "But first, we need some dinner. Let's get cleaned up then go get some food."

She sighed. "You had me at dinner."

Chapter Nineteen

Holly said goodnight to Ray and shut the door when her phone rang. She rolled her eyes when Randolph's name popped up. "Hello, Mr. Gordon. Yes, I've finished the first floor and started the second today." She paused while he spoke, then almost dropped the phone. "Your daughter will be here this weekend to check on the progress? She wants to plan on where to put her possessions? Well, yes, I can accommodate her, but I still have the upper floors to get ready. I still have a lot of linens to wash." She waited again. "Yes, sir. I'll make sure to have one of the bedrooms ready for her."

She hung up and plodded to the living room and dropped on the couch. Merlin jumped in her lap and stared at her. She ran her hand down his back and stared at the fireplace. Her time alone with the house would be over this weekend. Lydia Gordon would be here and there wouldn't be time alone with Ray any longer either.

"Oh, Merlin, what do we do now? Lydia will be here and from what people tell me, she isn't the best person." She laid her head back. "We only have one week left. Why couldn't she wait until we were done before she showed up?"

Merlin meowed and rubbed his head on her chin. She scratched him behind his ears and his purr gave her the comfort she craved.

"I think I need to tell Ray about this. He might be able to help me figure how to handle the situation when she gets here." She moved the cat off her lap and stood. "House, we may have a huge problem. Lydia Gordon will arrive this weekend." The house almost shuddered when she told it. "I know. I need to talk to Ray and get his thoughts. I'll be back soon. Take care of Merlin for me."

She hurried down the street until she found Ray's car in a driveway. She walked up and knocked on the door. After several long seconds, she knocked again.

Ray looked surprised to see her. "Holly, what are you doing here? I thought you'd be ready for bed by now. Is there a problem with the house?" He ushered her inside and into his living room. "How can I help?"

"We have a big problem. After you left, Randolph called me. His daughter will be here this weekend to check on the progress of the house. She wants to plan when to move her stuff."

He ran a hand through his hair. "You're right. This is a big problem. I don't think we're ready for Lydia to arrive so soon. Let me make a phone call." He hurried to the kitchen and she heard him on the phone. He came back in and yanked his shoes on. "We're going to see Miss Dee and she said she'd call Mrs. Hall." He held his hand out and pulled her up from the couch. "Let's go."

They pulled into Warner's B and B parking lot at the same time as Mrs. Hall. They walked up to the front door together and Ray held the door open for the two ladies. Dee led them to the drawing room and they sat across from each other.

"Now, Holly, tell us what happened," Dee said.

She took a deep breath and let it out. "Randolph called me tonight. He said his daughter will be here this weekend to check out the house. This only gives me three days to get more rooms cleaned. I don't know what to do. The house isn't close to ready for her."

Mrs. Hall leaned forward, a twinkle in her eyes. "What else has upset you about her visit, Holly? You can say what you truly feel. We won't judge you."

"Her visit makes me feel like she's intruding on my territory." She rubbed her arms as Dee and Mrs. Hall nodded at each other. "I can't shake the thought that the house is mine and she shouldn't be there. I know I sound like a bad person, but I can't help it. Every time I think of someone else in the house besides me, my stomach ties itself up in knots."

Mrs. Hall took her hand. "The house is yours. We need to figure out how to make Randolph Gordon see it. I haven't had time to call him yet, but don't worry. I'll be in touch with him soon."

Holly sagged back against the couch, grateful when Ray held her hand. "I don't know what I'd do without you ladies. We'd better go and let you get some rest. I'm sorry to keep coming to you with my problems."

"Don't worry about it, dear," Dee said. "This is what friends are for. Now, you two, run along home. Adelaide and I need to discuss this further."

When Holly and Ray got back to his car, she grabbed him in a tight hug. "Thank you for not thinking I'm bananas."

He smiled at her. "You're welcome, and don't worry. I like bananas."

****

Dee poured herself and Adelaide some tea. "I didn't want to upset Holly, but Lydia's early arrival worries me more than I want to admit."

"Me too, Dee." Adelaide took a sip of her tea. "I think I need to contact Randolph as soon as possible. The Founders Day celebration has taken up a lot of my time this year. I'm not sure how it became so much bigger than all the others."

Dee smiled. "I'd bet it's because Holly is here. We all know in our hearts she's the new Keeper of the Keys. Once she finds the Master Key, her title will be formally declared. Without her and the magic she carries, all the doorways to the realms will be in danger. We have to find a way to make Lydia want to leave."

"If the girl is as stubborn as her father, it won't be an easy task to accomplish." Adelaide set her cup down. "What if Randolph comes here? I don't think the house or Holly is strong enough to fight him."

"Not alone, but don't forget. It appears both Holly and the house have formed an attachment to Ray Burnett. I think the three of them together can take on Randolph and Lydia Gordon and win. But you know what I always say."

"I know, Dee. All will work out the way it's supposed to." They clinked their teacups and drank. "Whatever the outcome, Garland Falls is in for a big change on the horizon."

"I know. Let's hope the change will be for the best."

****

Holly walked into the house after Ray dropped her off. She leaned against the wall and let the tears she held back slip down her cheeks. She didn't want a

147

stranger to be in her house, even if Lydia had a stronger claim than she did. She couldn't help but feel the house belonged to her and her alone. Well, it would belong to her and Ray. She knew the house wanted them, too.

"Henrietta, tell me what to do. I don't want Lydia Gordon in our house, but how can I stop her? She's your family and I'm the actual stranger here." She dragged herself to the living room and collapsed on the couch. "I feel so lost right now. I know the vision you showed me had me and Ray here together. Right now, I don't see how it's possible."

She blinked and appeared back in Henrietta's bedroom. "Thank you for seeing me."

The ghost smiled. "Shouldn't I tell you that? I didn't expect my brother to send his horrible daughter here so soon. I thought we'd have more time. I wish I could tell you where to find the Master Key. If you held the key, he wouldn't have a claim to this house."

Holly sighed. "I wish I could find it, too. What if Lydia finds it while she's here? She'll turn it over to her father as fast as possible." Her eyes widened and she turned to Henrietta. "Could it be why she'll be here early? Did he send her to find the key? He's so anxious to get his hands on it."

Henrietta floated by the window. "You may have the right idea." She turned to Holly. "Trust me when I say she won't find it. The key is meant for you and you alone. The Red Cap man behind the purple door knew who you were the moment he saw you. You are the new Keeper of the Keys. I know you'll find it soon."

"I hope so. I'm curious to know what it looks like and what's behind all the colored doors around here."

"And there will be more doors for you to find when

you hold the Master Key." Henrietta's voice became distant as she started to fade. "Good luck, Holly. The house and I will watch over you."

Holly blinked and woke up on the couch in the living room. Merlin perched on her chest as he stared at her with his know-it-all look. She chucked him under his chin and smiled. "You know what, buddy? I think everything will turn out all right in the end after all."

Chapter Twenty

Holly rose before the sun to clean the carpeted staircase. She sat back on her heels and yawned. Merlin watched her from the second-floor landing. "I know I shouldn't be up this early, buddy. I didn't sleep well last night. I'm worried about Lydia Gordon's visit."

As soon as she voiced her fears, the house shuddered and threw her off balance once again. Merlin meowed and the house settled down. She had to smile. Her cat and the manor got along as well as her and the house.

"We've got to get one of the bedrooms done today and a bathroom." Holly worked for a few more minutes, then stopped and leaned against the banister. "I wish she wouldn't come here. I know it's wrong, but I feel more than ever this house is mine and I resent her already."

She went back to work and tried to scrub those thoughts from her mind. She'd never been possessive of any house before. Once again, her stomach soured, and she broke out in a cold sweat at the thought she'd have to leave soon. The house on Darkling Street belonged to her and no one would take it from her.

She finished the first flight of stairs and washed the wall up to the second floor. The new appliances had been delivered and hooked up. The chimney crew had arrived that morning and only had to do a few repairs but cleaned out a lot of debris. The bathrooms were done and sparkled when the lights were on.

The more she became attached to the house, the harder and faster she worked. She wanted her home to be restored to the wonderful place she knew it would be. She went back through the living room, dining room, kitchen, study, and library. With the windows clean and open, the atmosphere had changed. Holly smiled as she ran her fingers over the furniture in every room.

"You feel better now, don't you?" She could almost hear the house answer her. "I still have a lot of work to do on the upper floors, but at least the hard level is done. We have to try to make Lydia Gordon realize you aren't for her."

Merlin walked down the steps and looked up at her. "You're right, buddy. Time to get back to work. We have to make sure we get the house ready for Ms. Gordon." She looked around the library. "Even if she doesn't deserve it."

Merlin meowed his agreement.

****

Mrs. Hall drummed her fingers on the desk while she listened to Randolph Gordon make his wishes known in a very loud voice. Could the man be quiet for two minutes?

"Randolph, you knew your sister's wishes before you left Garland Falls. If you wanted to make sure Lydia could take possession of her home, you should have returned and talked to her about it." She waited again while he spoke. "Don't you dare take that tone of voice with me, sir. Lydia is not the rightful heir to Henrietta's house. Holly Stevens is, and you know it. If you don't believe me, you haul your pretentious carcass down to your hometown and see for yourself."

Mrs. Hall slammed the phone down and muttered under her breath about Randolph Gordon's foolishness. She knew Holly would be in for a hard time with Lydia, but Holly had a strong spirit. She didn't think Lydia would be able to bully her or push her out of the house before the thirty days were up.

Maybe she should pay a visit to the house on Darkling Street. Holly might be in need of some company right about now, whether she knew it or not. Her course of action decided, Mrs. Hall grabbed her purse and climbed in her car. It didn't take long to get there. It never took long to get anywhere in the small town. She pushed through the iron gates and knocked on the front door.

"Mrs. Hall," Holly said, unable to suppress the surprise in her voice. "I didn't expect to see you today. Please come in."

Mrs. Hall walked in and smiled as she looked around. "You've worked wonders on this place and in such a short time. The woodwork hasn't shined like this since Henrietta lived here. The hardwood floors are as beautiful now as they were back in the day." She paused and inhaled deeply. "Did you use actual beeswax? It smells wonderful." She smiled when Holly nodded. "My mother used beeswax when she cleaned. Do I smell lemon under the honey?"

"Yes. It's my mother's formula but I tweaked it a little. I use a combination of different oils combined with the beeswax to bring out a deeper shine. I also throw in a little lavender to have a calm scent underneath. My mother never used lavender, but I love it. Do you like it?"

"Yes, I do, very much. It sounds like the same formula my mother used." She gave Holly a conspiratorial smile. "Are you sure you don't have any ties to Garland Falls?"

She chewed her bottom lip before she formed an answer. "My mother did say she had a distant cousin who lived in the northern Midwest. She said she got the formula from her."

"Holly dear, there is a slight possibility we might be related."

They walked into the living room and sat on the leather couch. "It would explain the sense of déjà vu I had when I first arrived here. Mrs. Hall, the more I work on this house, the more possessive I've become of it. I don't want Lydia here. What is wrong with me? I shouldn't feel this way, should I? I mean, is this house evil, like something out of a horror movie?"

"The house isn't evil, and it doesn't want to possess you. It wants you as the new Keeper of the Keys." She watched as Holly got up to pace. "I can confirm you are perfectly fine."

"But I've never felt like this with any of the other houses I worked on. Why this one? Is it because of the magic Miss Dee claims I have? Does the house need magic to, I don't know, survive?"

Mrs. Hall frowned at the worry on Holly's face. The child feared the changes happening in her. "Sit down, dear." She waited until Holly plopped down next to her. She took her hand and gave it a brief squeeze. "You and the house are good. If there were any evil here, I wouldn't have come. You've brought light and love back in. Yes, you have magic. Yes, it will take time for you to understand what it is and what it means. Believe me, you don't have to worry or be afraid. We'll all be here to help you."

"What about Lydia Gordon? I don't think I have any right to fight her or keep her from the house." She paused, then looked up at Mrs. Hall. "Do I? I mean if she's as nasty as you all say she is, should I keep her from the house?"

"I'm afraid I don't know the answer to that, my dear girl." Mrs. Hall gave her hand a final squeeze. "See if you can talk to Henrietta. She might be able to help you a little more than I can with her niece." Merlin sauntered in and jumped in Mrs. Hall's lap. "So, this is your guardian I've heard so much about. Hello, my good sir."

Merlin meowed and stood on his hind legs which brought him nose to nose with Mrs. Hall. The two stared at each other before he rubbed his head against her chin. She laughed and petted him. "I think I have the gentleman's approval. I like you too, Merlin." She studied him. "You know, he looks very familiar. The town had a cat who wandered around who looked like him. One day, he disappeared."

"It couldn't be Merlin," Holly said. "I found him on my porch in my town in Vermont. He was only six weeks old and underfed. We've been together for the last three years. This guy is my buddy. He goes with me everywhere."

Merlin cocked his head as Mrs. Hall continued to look at him. "I think this young man has almost as many secrets as this house. Do you have a magical secret of your own, you pretty boy?" She put the cat off to the side when he meowed and rubbed his head on her chin again, and stood. "I thought so. I'd best get back to my office. I still have a lot of work to do for the Founders Day festival. I do hope you'll attend."

"I make my own schedule, so I'll be sure to come. I'll ask Ray to come with me." She hesitated. "Do you speak cat and if so, can you teach me?"

"You'll understand him soon," Mrs. Hall said before she hugged her. "An invitation to Ray is a wonderful idea. If he gets out with more people in town, they'll come to see what we already know."

Holly smiled. "They'll know he's a good man and they won't treat him as badly as they did in the past."

"And you are the young lady to change their attitudes. You're very important to Garland Falls, Holly. You'll soon find out how much."

Chapter Twenty-One

Thursday arrived quicker than Holly wanted, and that meant Lydia Gordon would be here the next day. Why couldn't she find Henrietta? Why did the ghost always disappear when she needed her the most? Lydia would invade her space sooner rather than later and it set her teeth on edge. Ray had worked hard on the yard, but the back gave him a whole new set of problems. The grass had grown too high and too thick.

She picked up Merlin when he rubbed against her ankles. "I don't suppose you've talked to Henrietta, have you? No? Well, I haven't been able to spend any time with Ray. Lydia's visit has already cramped our style and she's not even here yet, you know?"

This time, Merlin answered her with a quiet growl and a sneeze. Holly scratched his chin. "Allergic to Lydia Gordon already? Me too."

The flower beds were still empty. Ray had told her he needed to take some soil samples to make sure he got the right plants in the ground. Holly decided to go to Callahan's Floral Emporium to get fresh flowers to place around the house. Just because she didn't want the interloper, didn't mean the house shouldn't look its best. She put Merlin on the couch and grabbed her keys.

The bell over the shop door chimed as she walked in. She inhaled the scents of rose, lilac, lavender, and others she couldn't name. She thought the combined aromas would be strong, but they all blended together, and brought back memories of her mother's perfume. Her mother had changed perfumes frequently in recent days, and Holly missed the one she used to smell as a child.

"Holly, what a pleasant surprise," Ray said as he hurried out from behind the counter. "What can I help you find?"

"I need some fresh flowers to decorate the house." She grinned. "I also wanted to see you. We've worked so hard on the house we haven't had time to say two words to each other. Time is in short supply now and Lydia will be here soon. I'd like the house to look its best."

"Lucas said he'll let me borrow the big mower to tackle the backyard. I'll have it done tonight. As soon as I get the soil sample results, I'll know what to plant in the gardens."

They both turned when Lucas came out of the back room. "Holly, how nice to see you again. Did you come to steal Ray away?"

She laughed. "As much as I'd like to, no. I need bouquets for the house. Lydia Gordon arrives soon, and fresh flowers always make a house feel like a home."

"I tell you what. If you come clean my house when you're done on Darkling Street, I'll give you the bouquets for free. I'll even let Ray off at lunchtime to give you some extra help today. Deal?"

"Lucas, your generosity knows no bounds. Thank you and of course it's a deal. I'll be happy to come work at your house."

The two men brought bouquets to the counter. "By the way," Lucas said. "I talked to my brother, and we'll be over this weekend to sand and paint the fence. Of course, Ray will be happy to help too, won't you?"

Ray grinned. "I work for you, so I do what you say."

"And don't you forget it. Now, why don't you help Holly take these out to the house," Lucas said as they loaded the bundles into Holly's car. "When you get back, go ahead and get the big mower and get to work on her backyard. It's not too busy in here today. I can handle it."

"Thanks, Lucas. You're a great boss."

Lucas clapped him on the shoulder. "If you want to try and butter me up to get a raise, it might work. Hit the road, you two. I'll see you tomorrow, Ray."

Holly walked to her car, Ray right behind her. "I guess I'll see you at the house."

"I'll see you there," he said.

Holly pulled up at the manor and carried in the flowers. Merlin waited on the bottom step and meowed his usual greeting. "Make yourself useful, buddy. Find me some vases for the flowers."

The cat jumped off the step and stalked into the kitchen. He bypassed the pantry door to another smaller door hidden from view. He sat down and placed his paw on it. Holly looked at him and shrugged. She opened the door and found a small cupboard filled with all types of vases.

"I don't even want to know how you knew how where find this." He looked at her and walked back to the living room. "One of these days, I will learn how to speak cat," she murmured.

She carried six vases to the sink and scrubbed them out. They sparkled in the afternoon light as she dried them and set them on the table. Soon, the rumble of a mower filled the kitchen. She gazed out the window and saw Ray starting the backyard. The large machine made the work easy to take down the large weeds and several small saplings.

How could he do such a mundane task and still make her heart flutter in her chest? How could he still be the handsomest man she'd ever seen even though he wore headphones and safety goggles? She knew the reason deep down in her bones. She'd fallen head over heels in love with him. She put the last vase down when she felt the familiar touch of Henrietta's contact hit her.

She opened her eyes and smiled when she stood in the woman's bedroom. "I'm so glad you contacted me, Henrietta. I worried I wouldn't be able to talk to you before your niece arrives."

"I'm sorry I couldn't give you the advice you sought. Adelaide gave as good advice as I could have done, though."

"I wanted to ask you if you ever felt possessive of the house when you were alive. The more I work here, the more I don't want to leave." She walked to the window and watched Ray cut the grass. "I don't want Lydia here. Her presence strikes me as an invasion. Does that make me a bad person?"

"Of course not." The ghost floated next to her; the cold around her made Holly shiver. "I don't want her here either. I know Adelaide called Randolph and told him about my wishes, but I don't think it did any good. My brother is a strong-willed man. He always gets his way, no matter who he hurts."

"Why does your brother have to be so awful to everyone?" Holly turned back to watch Ray work.

"What can I do?"

"We'll have to see." Henrietta smiled as she glanced at Holly. "Ray Burnett is a very handsome man, isn't he?"

"Yes. I've known him for almost three weeks." She turned to Henrietta. "Is love at first sight possible?"

"When it comes to love and magic, it's all possible." They both turned when a loud knock echoed through the house. "You had best see who's here."

Holly came back to herself and headed to the front door. She opened it and a tall, thin woman with a hatchet face stood there and glared at her. Her blue eyes held no warmth or welcome, her cheeks as hollow as her gaze. Her lips were a thin, red slash in her face. Her black dress hid any kind of a figure she may have had and hung an inch below her knees. She wore black low-heel pumps and too many rings and bracelets. Perfume assaulted Holly's senses and she fought the urge to not pinch her nose shut.

"Can I help you?"

"I'm Lydia Gordon." She pushed her way into the house. "How long until you're done with my house and I can move in?"

"I thought you weren't scheduled arrive until tomorrow," Holly said, as she tried hard to keep her voice neutral. The heavy scent of patchouli set off her gag reflex and she had to take a step back from Lydia. "I have another week of work to do. I started the second floor this week and I still have the third floor to do. There's an attic and I'm sure your aunt had boxes up there. I can clean it if you like. Would you want to go through the cartons to see if you want to save certain items?"

"I wouldn't keep any of this junk except maybe the couch. My father picked it out you know." Lydia glared at her down her long, pointed nose. "You're paid to clean the entire house. The attic is part of the house, is it not? Then I expect you to take care of it. Pick up my suitcase and show me to my room."

Holly ground her teeth at the woman's superior attitude. "Yes, ma'am. If you'll follow me?" *This woman is so lucky I don't have a mean streak.*

She walked up the stairs and almost had to drag the excessively heavy bag, Lydia right behind her. She fought the urge to turn around and tell the woman to back off. She didn't need this uppity woman breathing down her neck. She had cleaned the other room on the floor with its own bathroom. Every person she'd talked to was right. Lydia Gordon turned out to be one nasty woman. From the tremors she felt, the house didn't like her either.

She put the suitcase on the wooden chest at the foot of the bed while Lydia surveyed the room. "I'll leave you to unpack."

Lydia swung around and glared at her. "Shouldn't you unpack for me?"

"Ms. Gordon, I run a house cleaning service. I'm not your personal maid. I'm sure you can unpack your clothes yourself. There's food in the kitchen if you're hungry. If you'll excuse me, I need to get back to work."

"No, I don't excuse you."

Holly gave her a small smile. "Well then, I guess *you* have problem. Good afternoon, Ms. Gordon."

Holly forced herself not to slam the door. She stomped down the steps and grumbled under her breath.

How dare the woman treat her like a nineteenth century servant? She hoped she could get Lydia to leave within the next couple of days. She walked to the kitchen and Ray stood at the sink drinking a glass of water.

"Lydia Gordon is here early and she's a real piece of work," Holly said as she stood next to him. "People were right when they told me how nasty she is. I don't think we'll get along, considering I want to shove her out the door."

He nodded. "I saw a new car in the driveway when I came in for a drink. What's she like?"

Holly rolled her eyes. "I've met nicer snakes at the zoo."

He chuckled. "Wow. Sounds like a real winner you've got here."

"She made me carry her suitcase upstairs and then expected me to unpack for her." She couldn't stop the groan that climbed its way out of her throat. "She may be an adult, but she's such a spoiled brat."

Ray put his arm around her shoulders and kissed the top of her head. "Don't let her get to you. She'll be gone before you know it."

"I hope you're right," she said as she crossed her fingers.

Chapter Twenty-Two

Ray went back outside to finish the yard as Holly washed out his glass. She heard footsteps on the stairs and cringed. "I'm not ready for another confrontation with this woman," she mumbled.

"Ms. Stevens," Lydia barked out.

Holly took a deep breath and turned around. "What do you want now?"

"Please prepare some lunch for me and bring it to my room. I'm exhausted."

She put the glass in the cabinet and said, "You can't be too exhausted if you walked down the stairs. There's stuff in the refrigerator for sandwiches. The silverware is in this drawer here. I think you can manage. As I said before, I have work to do."

Lydia's eyes narrowed as her sunken cheeks reddened. "I will not have you speak to me like this. And I wouldn't have had to walk down all those stairs if there were a reliable call system in place in this mausoleum."

Holly took two steps toward her. "Then I suggest you keep a civil tone when you talk to me. I'm not your servant, your significant other, or your family. I don't have to listen to your nastiness. You're a grown woman. I'm pretty sure you can make your own food. If you can't, go to one of the restaurants in town. I'm not paid to wait on you hand and foot."

"I'll be sure to tell my father about your bad attitude. You'll be fired in a minute."

Holly laughed. "Go ahead. Then you can finish cleaning this house by yourself. You won't hurt me in the least. I'm sure you've cleaned lots of houses, haven't you?"

She walked out of the kitchen and left Lydia standing there with her mouth hanging open. Holly bet no one had ever refused to bow to her whims before. She smiled, pleased to be the first to tell her off. Silent laughter surrounded her, and she didn't know if it came from Henrietta or the house itself. Either way, the three of them were happy.

She grabbed her cleaning supplies and started on the other rooms on the second floor. She'd have to haul the steam vac up here to make sure the carpets were as clean as she could make them. When she heard the front door slam, she took the opportunity to do the rug in Lydia's room. The old witch would never know she'd been in there.

Holly worked for over an hour in one room when she heard a car return. Lydia's screechy voice reached her. What did the woman need help with now? "Sorry, Ms. Gordon. I can't hear you."

She continued to vacuum and ignored the woman downstairs. When she finished, she unplugged the machine and took her time going to see what upset her unwelcome guest. Lydia pointed at Merlin who sat on the bottom step and looked pleased with himself. He groomed his front paw and ignored the woman who screamed in front of him.

Holly sat next to him on the steps and ran her hand down his back. "Don't tell me you're afraid of one little cat?"

"You call this monster little? Does my father know you brought a wild animal into his house?"

Holly rose to her feet and frowned. She took a deep breath in an effort not to shout. "Merlin is not a 'wild animal,' and yes, I asked your father's permission to bring him and he gave it."

"Get your beast out of here or I'll have him removed."

Holly walked closer until they were almost nose to nose. "Try it and you'll be the one removed. Touch my cat and you'll wish you never came to Garland Falls. And let me tell you this. Your aunt owned this house, not your father, so it's hers. Got it?"

Lydia moved a half step closer. "This house is Gordon property. You're the trespasser."

"No, I'm not. Your father invited me, and paid me to be here." She picked up Merlin and started up the stairs. "Don't bother me again. If you want to move in on time, I need to finish my work."

Holly took Merlin into the first bedroom with her and put him on the bed. "Can you believe the nerve of her? I'll be glad when I don't have to deal with Lydia Gordon anymore."

Merlin meowed his agreement.

****

Ray finished the backyard and groaned at how much needed to be edged. The yard looked a lot smaller when the grass was high. The manor's yard matched the house it surrounded. He walked around to the front and decided edging out here would be as much work as the back, if not more. There were the gardens, the sidewalk, not to mention around the fence.

He looked up at the house. It needed a fresh coat of paint. It meant he needed to find someone with a power washer and a ladder to get all the way up to the roof. He shook his head. And Holly thought the inside would take a long time. If he could get Lucas and his brother and maybe some other people, they could have the outside done in three days, four at the most.

He walked up to the front door and knocked. He had to let Holly know how much more he needed to do. He stepped back when a strange woman opened the door. The predatory gleam in her eye as she stared at him made his hands tremble. Her tall, skeletal frame looked like she'd break in a strong wind. Her long nose looked out of place on her narrow face. Her pointed chin reminded him of some of the fairies in the Dark Lands. Time to state his business and get the heck out of here.

"I need to speak with Holly Stevens. Is she around?"

The woman glanced over her shoulder. "I'm Lydia Gordon. Whatever you need to tell her, you can tell me. This is my house now. She went somewhere upstairs with her crazy cat." She opened the door wider. "Please come in and tell me what I can do for you."

Besides leave me alone? He tried to move away inch by inch, so Lydia wouldn't notice. "She hired me to take of the outside cleanup. Can you get her, please?"

Lydia took him to the living room and pushed him down on the couch. She sat close to him, a little too close for his comfort. "I'll pay for whatever you think is necessary. Why don't you let me take you out to dinner tonight and you can tell me all about it."

"I…uh…I mean…"

"Ms. Gordon," Holly shouted. "What do you think you're doing?"

Lydia glared at Holly as she slowly unfolded herself from the couch. "I wanted to talk to your handsome handyman. I think I should be the one to do all the negotiations with him. Why don't you go back to your maid duties."

Merlin stood next to Holly and growled deep in his throat at Lydia, and she backed up a step.

Ray had never been so happy to see someone or some cat in his entire life. He shot to his feet, glad to put distance between himself and the overbearing Lydia. "Ms. Stevens, I've made some good progress on the yard. Would you like to come take a look and we can go over the other expenses for the rest of what needs to be done."

"Ms. Gordon," Holly said. "I've told you to watch how you talk to me. Why don't you go take up space somewhere else while I tend to business. Come, Mr. Burnett. Show me what needs to be repaired outside."

She grabbed his arm and he blew out a breath, happy to be led away. "You know, if Lydia Gordon had moved another inch closer to me on the couch, I might have had to marry her," he said. "The woman has no idea about personal space."

"Trust me. I get it." They stood on the walkway and faced the house. "All right, what do you think still needs to be done out here."

He pointed out how much edging needed to be done. "The grass needs to be pulled from the cracks, and the house needs to be power washed before it can be repainted. Lucas and Parker will be here this weekend to help me with the fence. I'm sure we can get it all done in less than a week."

"Good, because September twenty-second will be here before we know it. The yard looks a hundred percent better even though you aren't done yet. I can't wait to see what flowers you plant. The sooner we get it all done, the better." She glanced at the house and frowned. "Because if I have to put up with Lydia Gordon any longer than necessary, you might end up visiting me in jail."

He grinned. "You don't strike me as the violent type."

"I'm not usually, but she's been here less than eight hours and I'm already sick of her attitude. She needs a serious lesson in manners."

"You handled her pretty well inside. I think you can deal with whatever she'll throw at you." He chuckled. "Maybe you should invite Mrs. Hall and Miss Dee to meet her."

"Thanks for the vote of confidence and maybe I will. Those ladies will put her in her place." She sighed. "You'd better get on the yardwork while I get back to the inside work. Oh, and you'd better warn Lucas about how she hit on you. She might try with him or his brother, even though they're married."

He nodded. "Duly noted. Let's get to work."

He watched as Holly walked back inside and shook his head. He couldn't decide who he felt sorry for—her or Lydia Gordon or Merlin. He walked around back and climbed on the mower. Time to take it back to the nursery and get the heavy-duty edger. He glanced back at the house and cringed when Lydia smiled and waved to him.

He grinned. Time to go and let Lucas know what he could expect over the weekend.

Chapter Twenty-Three

When Holly saw Lydia's obvious flirtation with Ray, she almost threw a nearby vase at the woman. Poor Ray looked uncomfortable and ready to bolt if she moved an inch closer to him. The woman had some nerve to hit on her man. She stopped and stared at herself in the mirror she'd finished cleaning. Her man? Yes. In no time at all, Ray had become her man and the wicked witch in her house better stay away from him.

"Henrietta, if you can hear me, tell me how to get rid of this woman." The sensation she had become familiar with filled her and she found herself in Henrietta's bedroom. "Please tell me you have some plan to make her leave."

"Ray had the right idea. Invite Delia and Adelaide to come for a visit. She might guard her words a little more around those two." The ghost turned to her. "I'm sorry you have to deal with my terrible relation. I always found Lydia to be such a hateful child and Randolph spoiled her all the time. She has no idea how to be grateful."

Holly sank down on the bed. "If I could only find the Master Key. I'm sure it would negate any claim she or your brother would have on the house. The big problem is how to make them realize it."

Henrietta smiled at her. "Once you have the key, you'll have all the answers you want. I wish I could tell you how to get it. I think you have to find it without any help. It's the traditional way the Master Key is handed down. Everyone finds it in a different way. Whoever finds it first, they become the Keeper of the Keys."

"How did you find it?"

"I beat my brother in a treasure hunt. Our parents said the key would be the treasure. My parents were happy I became the new Keeper. My brother has a dark side to him. Some of our ancestors came from the Dark Lands. Sometimes, the dark side comes out. With Randolph, it came out more often than not."

"Ray said half of his heritage is from the Dark Lands. Could he turn dark, like your brother?"

Henrietta smiled. "I don't believe so. Strife fell head over heels in love with Ray's mother. Ray's love for you matches his parents' love for each other. It overpowers any dark tendencies he fears he may have. If there was the slightest possible chance he'd turn dark, the house wouldn't have accepted him. He's supposed to be here with you."

"If we could only get rid of Lydia." Holly grinned as a thought struck her. "You know, I could get more cats."

Henrietta laughed. "Yes, that might be one way, but I think Merlin wouldn't approve of your plan."

"True and I don't want to upset him. He's such a good boy."

Henrietta began to fade. "You'd best get back to work. She may search you out soon. Do keep her in her place. The house and I have enjoyed your feistiness."

Holly blinked and came back to herself in the room where she worked. She conceded Henrietta's advice. She needed support from Dee and Adelaide. She grinned when she remembered Henrietta called her feisty. She guessed she could be when the situation called for it. Now, how to find a key no one knew where it could be hidden or when it would be found.

****

Ray returned the mower then drove to town hall. The elders needed to know about Lydia Gordon's arrival. If the mayor said one word wrong to him, he'd stand up for himself and to heck with the consequences. He always tried to be invisible to the people who mistrusted him, but he'd taken Holly's words to heart. He needed to let everyone know he wouldn't be stepped on or insulted any longer.

He knocked once on the mayor's door, then walked in without waiting for the invitation to enter. "Mayor, Lydia Gordon has arrived a day early. She's out at the house on Darkling Street right now. Holly Stevens is still there, also, and the two don't get along."

"Burnett, how dare you come in before I tell you to enter."

Ray shrugged. "Listen, if you don't want me to tell you about what the Gordons have planned, fine." He walked over to the mayor's desk and leaned on it. His nearness made the other man shrink back in his chair. "If you want any more cooperation out of me, you'll treat me with a little more respect or you can kiss all I learn goodbye." He straightened up and stared at the town elders. "I've said my piece. Do with it what you want."

He turned on his heel and stalked from the office, and for the first time, slammed the door behind him. It felt as good as he knew it would. He saw Mrs. Hall walk toward the mayor's office. "Hi, Mrs. Hall. Do you need to see the mayor?"

"Yes. We need to finalize the last few details for the Founders Day celebration." She stared at him and narrowed her eyes. "You look different."

"Oh? I'm not sure what you mean. I haven't changed my appearance. I'm the same as I've always been."

"I don't think that's quite true." Her eyes narrowed as she walked around him. "Your posture is better, you're not all hunched over like usual. Your confidence has gone way up." They heard loud voices come from the mayor's office. "And from the chaos I hear in there, you stood up to the mayor and his cronies. Good for you, by the way."

"Yes, ma'am, I did. I came to tell them Lydia Gordon arrived a day early. Holly and I wanted to invite you and Miss Dee out to meet her. We both think she needs to be given a huge reality check." He grinned and winked at the stout older lady. "Would you two be interested?"

Mrs. Hall rubbed her hands together. "Oh, we're interested all right. I'll call Dee as soon as I finish my business with the mayor." She pulled him down to kiss his cheek. "I'm so happy for you, Ray. It's about time you made people realize they can't hurt you any longer. Tell Holly we'll be out early this evening."

Ray whistled as he walked out to his car. Holly did have magic and it worked on him. He no longer cared what the townspeople thought of him. He had friends here, Garland Falls itself didn't have a problem with him, and now he had Holly. Could his life get any better than this?

He drove back to the nursery. If only they could

find the Master Key. He rolled his eyes. If they kicked Lydia Gordon out of the house on Darkling Street, that would be great, too.

He strolled into the store. "Lucas, I'm back."

His boss came out of his office. "I thought you went to Holly's to get more work done."

"I'm headed over there in a few minutes. I need to grab the good edger. There's a lot of property to clean up." They walked out to the tool shed. "I also had some news to tell the mayor." He selected the edger he needed and turned to Lucas. "Lydia Gordon is here a day early and nastier than ever."

"Oh, yippee for us," Lucas said as he rolled his eyes.

Ray grinned. "Yep, and she hit on me right in front of Holly. I thought my girl would explode."

"Your girl?"

Ray nodded. "I can't fight it. Holly's my girl and she told me to warn you. Once Lydia sees you and Parker, you might be subjected to the same flirtations. Maybe you should invite your ladies to come out with you."

Lucas laughed. "I can picture her face when our wives would get out of the car. Let's see her try to take on my girl. She'll end up with a broken arm."

"Then she'd hit on Sean at the hospital. We wouldn't want to put him through that, would we?"

"I guess not."

The two laughed as they walked out to Ray's car and put the edger in the trunk. Ray opened his door. "So, we'll see you two this Saturday?"

"You bet. I wouldn't miss this for the world." Lucas rubbed his chin. "Maybe we can hurry her decision to leave. Let me talk over some ideas with Parker. See you later, Ray."

As he drove back to the manor, Ray did feel a little sorry for Lydia. He knew Lucas' sense of humor. He and his brother caused so much trouble when they were children. If Lydia didn't behave herself, she'd be in for a rough time this weekend.

****

"You might as well know right now, Ray is off limits to you," Holly said.

Lydia sat on the couch, a smug smile on her thin lips. "What makes you think you can tell me what to do? You boss him around like he's beneath you. I could make him very happy."

"I've had it. I've heard enough out of you, lady." Holly glared at her as she marched toward the couch. "You might as well know right now Ray and I are together. We got engaged earlier this week. You don't have a chance with him."

Lydia unfolded her spindly frame off the couch to loom over Holly. "You're a liar. You're the one with no chance. I have money, mansions, and a father who dotes on my every whim. I can give him all he could ever want. What are you?" She snorted. "A glorified maid with no money and no options. I'm better than you in every way, you little nobody."

"True, you have all you said and I work hard, sometimes harder than I should." Holly stepped closer. "But you have an ugly soul, Lydia. Ray wouldn't want you if you were the last woman on Earth. Now, I have to get back to work. I have one week left on my contract and two more floors to do. Stay out of my way, Ms. Gordon. I won't tell you again."

Holly turned on her heel and stomped up the stairs as Merlin scurried up behind her. "You know what, buddy? I think I'd better tell Ray I said we're engaged. I hope he doesn't freak out."

Chapter Twenty-Four

Holly went out of her way to avoid Lydia. The woman barked orders at her all the time. Merlin stayed closer than usual to her and hid in their room whenever Lydia came near.

"Ms. Stevens," Lydia bellowed from downstairs. "Come down here this instant."

Holly looked at Merlin and grinned. "What do you think? Should I just ignore her like I have since yesterday?" When he stuck his tongue out, she sighed. "You're right. She'll just yell until I see what she wants. Wish me luck."

She walked down to the first floor and saw Lydia standing by the oak cabinet she'd pushed in front of the purple door. Ever since she moved it, the door hadn't made a sound. At least the floor didn't get scratched from its square feet. Lydia tapped her foot and folded her arms. This would be a fun conversation.

"What do you want now?" Holly said. "If you keep interrupting me, you won't have a fully clean house to take over."

"Why is this cabinet in front of a door? Are you hiding stolen goods in there?"

Holly rolled her eyes, not caring how rude it looked. "Are you kidding me? The latch is broken on the door and I didn't want my cat to go in until I had a chance to go through it. Why? Do you want to hide stolen items in there?"

"Typical of a thief to accuse an innocent person of the same crime. Move this back to where it belongs."

"No."

Lydia stepped closer to her. "I am the owner of this house and you will do as I say." She folded her arms and glared at her. "Now, move it."

Holly laughed. "Are you trying to intimidate me, because it's not working." She tapped her finger on the cabinet. "I'll move it when I'm ready and not before. Now, I need to get back to work, something you know nothing about."

She turned on her heel and ran up the steps. She took several deep breaths to calm down. Lydia Gordon had the supreme ability to get under her skin in microseconds. Why did she let the woman get to her all the time? It was more than her bad attitude. It was the way she constantly insisted the house was hers.

She went back to cleaning the room next to hers. She'd put Lydia down the hall in the only other room with a private bath. "Merlin, more than ever, I'm glad we put Lydia far away from us on this floor. She's driving me crazy with her superiority complex. I'm about ready to punch her lights out." Merlin meowed and sneezed. "Of course I wouldn't do it, but it's fun to think about. You know I've had to stand up for myself most of my life. I'm not about to start backing down now."

At noon, Ray pulled up and knocked. Holly hurried downstairs, but Lydia beat her to the door. "Why Mr. Burnett, do come in," she said, putting a tight grip on his arm. "Ms. Stevens, please get us some lunch. Mr. Burnett and I have so much to discuss."

"No, we don't," Ray said, prying her fingers off his arm. "I actually came to get Holly. We always have lunch together."

Lydia turned a smarmy smile to Holly as she latched onto Ray again. "Not today, you don't. Today, I insist on your company."

"Ms. Gordon, if you don't take your hands off my fiancé, you and I are going to have a major problem," Holly said. "Ray, wait for me outside."

"Gladly," he said, shaking off Lydia's talon fingers one more time. "I'll be in the car."

As soon as he left, Holly rounded on Lydia. "If you touch him or come near him one more time, I won't be responsible for anything I say or do. I told you before, we're engaged. If you have a problem with that, I suggest you leave Garland Falls and find your own man."

When Lydia raised her hand, Holly's own hand shot out. "If you hit me, I'll make sure you're arrested for assault. Now get out of my way. I'm ready for some lunch."

She pushed past the other woman and stomped out to Ray's car. She got in and he didn't say a word. He pulled out and took them straight to the diner. A parking spot opened up as they arrived, and he pulled in. He shut the car off and looked at her. She'd stared straight ahead the whole way to Sal's and didn't say a word.

"Correct me if I'm wrong, but I think you're angry," he said.

She sagged back in the seat. "I swear something bad is going to happen if I have to put up with her any longer than necessary. She's driving me crazy and if she touches you one more time…"

He reached out and squeezed her hand. "I get it, and don't worry. I'll try to keep as far away from her as possible." He paused and a slow smile spread. "Did you call me your fiancé or was I mistaken?"

Holly opened the car door. "I don't want to talk about it yet. Can we just get lunch?"

They entered the diner and the man who always got up and left when they arrived frowned at them. Her hands balled into fists and she frowned. "Why don't you just leave now so we don't have to put up with your nonsense," she said.

When he hurried out, they sat at the counter. Sally came over, an amused smile on her face. "You want to tell me what that was about?"

"I'm just not in the mood for people's attitudes today."

Sally gave them menus. "I heard Lydia Gordon is in town. I guess she's staying at the house on Darkling Street?"

Holly nodded. "Her attitude is stressing me out. What can you recommend to keep me out of jail?"

"We have a nice stew today and fresh biscuits. Comfort food is always perfect when you're out of sorts."

Ray handed her back the menus. "You've done it again, Sally. Your magic must be knowing what people need to eat to feel better."

She winked. "It's a gift."

"Is it bad I don't want to go back there and deal with Lydia anymore today?"

He shook his head. "No, it's not. She's a hard person to get along with. You want to work on the yard with me and stay away from her?"

She smiled at him as she buttered a biscuit Sally put in front of her. "I'd love to, but I have to finish the second floor. Next week is the last week of my contract and I still have the third floor to do. At least there's not as many rooms up there. If she wants the attic cleaned, she can do it herself."

"I thought you wanted to keep the house."

She ate her stew and asked for another biscuit. "I do, so when I take over, then I'll get to the attic. Since you'll be with me, you can help."

They finished and Ray drove them back to the house. Lydia stood on the porch, waiting for them. Holly groaned and rolled her eyes.

"You have got to be kidding me." She climbed out of the car and walked up to the house. "What now, Ms. Gordon?"

"I wanted to ask Mr. Burnett about other places to eat in this small town. There has to be more than that awful diner."

Holly looked back at Ray. "Can you handle this?"

"I'll be all right. Get back to work and I'll see you tonight."

She pushed past Lydia and headed straight for the second floor. Merlin dozed where she left him. "You are so lucky you're a cat."

He yawned and looked like he smiled at her.

Chapter Twenty-Five

A few days later, visitors knocked and Holly hurried to answer the door before Lydia could. If Ray stood on the porch, she didn't want the woman anywhere near him. She opened the door, delighted to see who had come.

"Miss Dee, Mrs. Hall, how nice of you to stop by." The overpowering scent of Lydia's perfume surrounded her and she knew the woman stood close behind her. "Ms. Gordon, I'd like you to meet two distinguished members of Garland Falls. This is Dee Warner, who runs the fabulous bed and breakfast up the hill. This is Mrs. Adelaide Hall. She's in charge of all the wonderful events in our town. Ladies, this is Lydia Gordon. She's here to take possession of this lovely old house."

As they shook Lydia's hand the two older ladies gave each other a side glance. "We're very happy to meet you, Ms. Gordon," Dee said. "You must love this old house as much as we do. Holly has done a wonderful job to clean it up and get it ready for you."

"Yes, but I'm sure someone else could have done a better job," she said, her words cold, her voice colder. "Ms. Stevens isn't as competent as I thought she'd be."

"Well, I'm sure she'll give it one more run through over before you take full possession, right, Holly?" Mrs. Hall said.

"Of course. We wouldn't want Miss High and Mighty here to be upset, would we?" Holly directed an overly sweet smile to Lydia, who stalked away.

The three laughed as Holly showed them into the living room. "So, what do you think of our new arrival?" Holly said.

"She's twice as nasty now as a grown woman than she was as a child," Dee said. "No wonder Henrietta didn't want her to have her house. I'm surprised you haven't booted her out."

"I wanted to do that and more when she hit on Ray. Can you believe her?" Holly chewed her lip and lowered her eyes. "I told her Ray and I are engaged. Then I called him my fiancé in front of him. He asked me about it, but I didn't want to talk about it. Do you think he'll be mad?"

"Did he want Lydia's attentions?" Mrs. Hall asked. Holly shook her head. "Then I think he'll be relieved to find out he's been taken off the market."

Dee leaned forward. "Do you realize when you talked about Garland Falls, you said 'our town?' "

"I did? No, I didn't realize. I think I do want to stay here. The people are so nice, except for the ones who insult Ray to his face. Those people will need an attitude adjustment."

Mrs. Hall chuckled. "I think Ray can take care of himself from now on. He stood up to the mayor this afternoon, and it was wonderful for me to hear. Poor old Theodore has no idea what to do with himself now."

Holly's eyes lit up and she grabbed Mrs. Hall's hand. "He told the mayor off? I'm so happy to hear some good news. What a wonderful way to brighten my day."

"We think you've been a good influence on him," Dee said.

"If only I could find the Master Key," Holly said. "I feel like all the answers hinge on its appearance. Henrietta said once I find it, everything will work out."

"She always knew what went on, even if she never made it clear how she came by the knowledge," Dee said.

A bloodcurdling shriek shot them to their feet. Merlin flew down the steps and ran into the room. Lydia stomped after him, as her ankle bled from deep scratches through her pantyhose. The cat leapt into Holly's arms, then turned and hissed at Lydia, and bared his teeth. Holly stroked and cooed to calm him down.

"I want this beast destroyed," Lydia screamed. "He attacked me for no reason."

Holly glared at her. "I doubt it very much. He's very even tempered. What did you do to my cat?"

"He wouldn't get out of my room, so I kicked at him. Then he scratched me. I know I'll get some dreadful disease from him."

"You kicked my cat?" Holly's body shook as she took slow, careful steps toward Lydia. "I've had it. You've been here for two very long days and you've upset me, Ray, and now Merlin. Get out of this house. You can come back when I've finished my work and not before. Miss Dee, will you take this mean-spirited, ungrateful…person…out of my house."

"Certainly," Dee said. She reached out and stroked Merlin, and let Adelaide do the same. "I'll send someone down for her luggage. Come, Ms. Gordon. I'll put you up at the B and B while Holly finishes cleaning the house."

"She wants to kick me out of my own house," Lydia screeched, "and you stand there and let her? And she called it her house?" She turned to Holly. "This is my house. You get out."

"It's not yours, not yet. Now would you please leave." She put Merlin on the floor, and Lydia backpedaled to the front door. "And if you come near my cat again, I won't be responsible for my actions."

"I'll be back tomorrow to make sure your yard crew gets here on time to get the job done. You can believe my father will hear about this and he'll make sure your cat is headed for kitty heaven." Lydia stopped on the walkway and turned around. "You hear me? You and your animal are done for in this town. The Gordons have returned and all of you will pay for the insult to me."

Holly slammed the door and looked down at Merlin, who looked mighty pleased with himself. "Good luck with your ridiculous threat, you brat."

When the afternoon quieted down, Holly ran her hands over Merlin's body to check for any damage Lydia may have done. "Well, buddy, you didn't whimper or flinch, so I think you're okay. Maybe I'd better find a vet and get a professional opinion."

Merlin voiced his agreement. She walked into the kitchen and gave him a handful of treats. He licked her hand and gobbled them up.

"The drama is over with now, let's get back to work." The house settled and the atmosphere cleared after Lydia had left. She ran her hand down the doorframe. "I bet you feel better too since we got rid of her."

Holly closed her eyes and felt relief settle over her. The house and Henrietta were both glad she kicked Lydia out. The manor belonged to Holly. She knew it deep down in her heart of hearts. This house belonged to her now and no one, not even the Gordons, would make her leave.

****

Ray pulled up as Dee drove away with Lydia Gordon in her car. He walked up to the porch and knocked on the door. He waited for a few minutes then pushed the door open and stepped inside. Peace filled him as he glanced in the living room, then the kitchen. Something major had changed because the house felt as calm as it used to before Lydia's arrival. Holly must be upstairs when he couldn't find her on the first floor.

"Holly? Are you here?"

"I'll be right down, Ray. I'm up to my elbows in dust bunnies."

While he waited, Merlin sauntered down the steps and rubbed against his ankles, and his purr vibrated Ray's legs. "Well, hello to you too, Merlin. Have you been keeping out of trouble with you-know-who?"

Holly walked down the steps. "You-know-who has been kicked out of my house. She tried to kick Merlin, so Miss Dee took her to the B and B. I won't have her here while I work."

Ray picked up Merlin. "He doesn't act like he's hurt."

"I checked him over, but I still want to have a vet look at him. Are there any in town?"

Ray thought for a moment. "We had one on Main Street, but he moved his office a little farther out of town. He's closed today so we can take Merlin there tomorrow before we start work."

"Thanks, Ray." She shuffled from foot to foot before, then looked up at him. "I do have some news to tell you, and it may come as quite a shock."

Ray put Merlin on the floor and rolled his shoulders. "Okay. I'm prepared. What's the big shock you need to tell me?"

"I told Lydia we were engaged."

Ray smiled when she told him. After all, he caught her calling him her fiancé the other day. Holly told Lydia they were engaged and he couldn't be happier. He stared at the woman who gave him her friendship, her smile, and her courage. He considered being engaged to Holly to be a great idea. Now, how to make it real and not a story for Lydia's benefit?

"Ray? Are you okay with a spur of the moment fiancée?"

He reached out and took her hands in his. Once again, their callouses lined up like they were made for each other. "I think an engagement to you is a great idea. My one regret is I didn't think of it first. And don't forget, you called me your fiancé once already, so I'd look foolish if I backed out now, wouldn't I."

She smiled and squeezed his hands. "I'm glad you aren't mad. I needed to tell her something to make her back off from you. Somehow, I don't think my news will stop her. She's the kind of person who always gets what she wants."

"Well, she won't get me. You have my word."

A sudden breeze blew through the house, and the curtains fluttered. The scent of lilac filled the hallway. Merlin batted at the curtains, and they laughed at his antics. After one final squeeze, Ray dropped her hands.

"We both have jobs we need to accomplish. We'd better get to it. Lucas and Parker will be here tomorrow to start on the fence." He opened the front door. "They know someone who can power wash the house and get a fresh coat of paint on the outside. Do you need to have the roof inspected?"

"It would be a good idea to have it done. The chimney crew came this past Monday and they gave it a clean bill of health."

Ray nodded. "Let's get to it then. See you in a little bit."

He walked out to his car and pulled out the edger. He wanted to start out front and around the manor's foundation. If cleaning the outside of the house would be after the yardwork, he wanted the crews to have a clear path to do the job. He put on safety glasses and headphones and got to work.

****

From the third-floor window, Henrietta gazed at Ray as he worked. Like almost every other couple, Ray and Holly were perfect together. The girl had ties to Garland Falls. She'd known about the distant connection between her and Adelaide Hall. She pushed her brother hard to get this particular girl here. Holly was the rightful heir to the house on Darkling Street. She would take her place as Keeper of the Keys.

Holly had the strength of spirit to help the Dark Landers on this street gain the acceptance they craved. Henrietta smiled as she remembered how Holly kicked Lydia out of the house and then claimed the property as her own. The crucial first step to Holly finding the Master Key had been taken.

Ray had become another integral part and she turned as Merlin appeared. "You, my brave boy, are the last piece of this very large puzzle. I hope Holly and Ray can stand against Randolph. I fear he'll show up in Garland Falls very soon."

Merlin meowed before he disappeared.

Chapter Twenty-Six

Saturday dawned bright and clear. Holly met Ray, Lucas, and Parker on the porch. "I appreciate your help and I'm sorry you had to come on your day off. I can't thank you enough."

"Far be it from us to deny a damsel in distress," Lucas said, while Parker nodded. "Let's get to work, guys. There's a lot of the fence for us to fix up."

As soon as they started, Miss Dee pulled up with Lydia Gordon in tow. She jumped out of the car and marched over to the men. Dee got out and stood by her car, with an amused smile.

Holly walked over and stood with her. "There's a lot of good-looking men here today. Poor Lydia doesn't stand a chance with any of them. When do the wives show up?"

"They want to give her a chance to embarrass herself before they put in an appearance. The Callahans have it all worked out. Did you tell Ray about your engagement statement yet?"

"Yes. I told him as soon as he got here. He thinks it's a great idea and said he should've thought of it first." She turned to the woman next to her. "You know, I think he wants to be engaged to me."

"It wouldn't surprise me in the least. You two were made for each other." Dee watched the interaction between Lydia and the men. "Adelaide tells me she thinks you might be a distant relation to her."

"My mother told me she had a distant cousin who lived here, but I'm not sure. I mean, Mom never talked about Garland Falls or any relations other than the ones who lived near us."

Dee tapped her fingers on her arm. "There have been a lot of people who've come here and have ties to this little town. It's like Garland Falls has called everyone home."

"I wonder why?" Holly said. "You haven't heard of any disasters in the future, have you?"

"Not as far as I know, but I'll ask around." She stood silent for several minutes. "It could be good for us. We've added some new people to the town and if long lost citizens have found their way back, it could be the town wants to strengthen the blood here."

"I love your positivity, Miss Dee." She turned her attention back to Lydia, who at the moment, looked very unhappy. "I think they told her they're married and it looks like Ray confirmed our engagement."

Dee nudged her. "Lydia Gordon is destined to find a man exactly like her."

"I wonder who I should feel sorry for. Lydia or the man who gets saddled with her."

They turned to each other and laughed.

****

"The dreadful woman hired to clean the house told you to lie, didn't she?" Lydia said. "You two aren't married." She turned to Ray. "And I know she lied about your engagement."

"I'm afraid it's all true, Ms. Gordon," Lucas said. "Parker and I are married, and Ray is engaged to Holly. Her name, by the way, is Holly, not any other derogatory name you want to call her."

Lydia crossed her arms and glared at them. "I demand you tell the truth, right now."

Ray laughed. "We did. It isn't our fault you don't believe us." They turned when a car pulled up. "There's Lucas' and Parker's wives now." All three men waved at the two women who walked toward Holly and Dee.

Lydia's mouth hung open. "You didn't lie?"

Ray frowned. "What kind of people do you hang out with to make you disbelieve everything you hear?"

She stepped close to Ray. "When my father arrives, he'll expose your engagement as the fraud I know it to be."

She stalked over to the group of women by Dee's car. "You," she shrieked at Holly. "You made Ray Burnett lie so I couldn't have him. You're an evil woman."

Lydia raised her hand to strike, and Holly flinched. Before anyone could react, another hand shot out and grabbed Lydia's wrist. "Hold it right there, lady. If you land that hit, I'll cart you off to jail so fast your head will spin."

"Who do you think you are?"

The woman flipped open a badge. "Agent Blair Callahan of the Holiday Security Agency. I am within my jurisdiction to keep the peace in Garland Falls. Now, if you don't want any trouble, I suggest you take yourself back to Warner's and not come down here again until you're invited. Understood?"

Lydia snatched her hand out of Blair's grasp and stalked toward her car. "All of you will be sorry you denied me what I declared to be mine."

As she sped off, Holly looked at the others. "I'm

sure Ray will be happy to know Lydia staked her claim on him."

The four of them laughed at the thought of Ray's reaction to Lydia's news.

****

After Dee and the others left, Holly went inside and got back to work. She'd finished the second floor and the third floor waited for her attention. She sighed. But she still had the attic to work on, and she still didn't know if she'd find a basement. The final days of the contract approached quickly, and she wanted to finish on time. Of course, it didn't matter since she didn't plan to leave.

On the third floor, there were five rooms, two on each side of the hallway and the one she knew led to Henrietta's bedroom. At the other end of the hall was the attic door. She opened the first door on her right and covered her nose and mouth. Stale air congealed in her lungs and made it hard to breathe. This room hadn't been opened in a long time. She crossed the room and opened the curtains. She shoved and struggled to open the window before it finally flew up.

Holly looked around the room. The décor claimed it as a nursery, and from the look of it, it had never been used. A crib stood against the far wall next to a changing table. A rocking horse and assorted toys were scattered around the room. Cute, painted animals lined the walls, along with trees, flowers, and butterflies. Henrietta appeared next to her, and Holly became overwhelmed by the ghost's grief.

"Henrietta, did your child grow up in this room?"

The ghost shook her head and floated over to the rocking horse. "I wanted to have children, to fill my home with the sound of their laughter. When we found out I couldn't get pregnant, my husband left me. I never used this room and changed back to my maiden name. I shut the pain away and have never entered here until today." She turned to Holly. "If the vision you had comes true, I want you to use this room for your children. The room next door is for the nanny. This is my gift to you."

"Oh, Henrietta, thank you so much. I hope my vision is right." The two women, one alive, one a ghost, stared at each other and smiled. "I'd better get to work."

Holly took extra time to restore the room to its past look. It took all day to make it perfect and she finished as the sun sank below the horizon. She'd have to work harder to make up the time she lost today. The last week of her contract had arrived and September twenty-second would arrive in two days. The house needed to be done by then, but she wasn't sure if it was for Randolph Gordon's benefit or for something else, something more important.

"Holly," Ray called from downstairs. "We're done for the night. We'll be back bright and early tomorrow."

"Wait, Ray. Can you come up here? I have a room I want to show you."

She listened to his footsteps get closer and smiled. When he reached the top, she took him into the nursery. "Henrietta designed this room for her children, but she couldn't have any. Isn't this a beautiful place?"

"It is and your work on it made it better." He put his arm around her shoulders. "You know, since I confirmed our engagement, this room could figure into our future."

Holly smiled up at him. "I love being engaged to you."

He kissed her forehead. "Then I suppose I'd better get you a ring so Lydia leaves me alone."

"Did you know she claimed you as her own?" she said as they walked down to the first floor.

Ray opened the front door. "This is proof she has no idea what she's talking about. Don't worry about her. We both know you staked your claim on me first."

"Yes, we do. Goodnight, fiancé."

"Goodnight, fiancée," he said.

Holly watched him drive away and shut the door. Merlin sat by her feet and looked up at her. "He's great, isn't he?" Merlin meowed. "I knew you'd agree. Come on, buddy. Let's get some rest. We've got another long day tomorrow and we still haven't found the Master Key. It's got to be here somewhere. Our deadline to be finished is almost here."

They climbed the stairs to their room. Merlin settled on the bed while Holly changed and climbed under the covers. As she snuggled down and let her eyes drift shut, she hoped to dream of Ray Burnett.

Chapter Twenty-Seven

Holly rose before the sun. Her dreams all night long predicted something special would happen soon. What it could be, she had no idea, but she couldn't wait. Maybe it would happen tomorrow. That was the autumnal equinox and the day she should have the house finished. An air of anticipation surrounded her as though the house itself couldn't wait to see what the future held.

She ate a quick breakfast and smiled at Merlin when he sauntered in. Ray had driven them out to the vet last evening and he confirmed what Holly suspected. Her buddy had no injuries because of the hateful woman who had wanted to hurt him.

At nine, Ray showed up with the Callahan brothers. She stood on the porch and waved to them. "Good morning, guys." She held up a familiar box. "Joanna from Heavenly Bites dropped off some cookies for a treat and Miss Dee said she'll be down with some cinnamon rolls in a little while."

The guys looked at each and grinned before Lucas let out a shout. Ray walked over to her. "He loves the cookies from Heavenly Bites. You had Parker at cinnamon rolls."

"And what do you like?"

He kissed her cheek. "Do you really need a serious answer to your question?"

"I guess not. I had some strange dreams last night. They weren't bad, but I feel they meant something important would happen tomorrow."

"Do you know what it is?"

She shook her head. "I guess we'll have to wait and see. You'd better get over there and get to work. I'll be on the third floor if you need me." She turned to go inside, then looked back. "Do you know anyone who can clean the outside of the upper story windows?"

"We can ask the power wash guys when they get here." He gazed up at the house. "Did you ever think you'd get this task done so fast?"

She shook her head. "It felt impossible when I first saw the house. But when I got started, it went quicker than I thought. I feel the house wanted to help me. Does that sound strange?"

He smiled. "It wouldn't be the weirdest occurrence in Garland Falls. I'd better get out there. See you in a bit."

Holly went back inside and heard a clank from the living room. Now, she knew the keyring had hit the floor again. She walked over to the keys and picked them up. "I thought we talked about this. You have to stay on the desk. I won't shut it if you want to see what's going on, but please don't fall on the floor anymore."

She placed the ring in the middle of the desk blotter and went back upstairs. She turned on her phone's music and let it get her into work mode. She'd finished the nursery the day before. She moved on to the room next to it and it did indeed look like the room of a nanny. She scrubbed and vacuumed and polished until the room glowed with renewed life.

She loved to make homes shine with light and life. To make a home gleam like it should gave her the greatest feeling in the world. She'd had no complaints from clients, even those who discontinued their service. She always got good reviews from everyone she worked for. She didn't worry about Lydia Gordon. If the bitter spinster said one bad word, she knew her reputation would stand against it.

She wiped her forehead and arched her back. She might have to have Ray stretch her out again. A commotion from the yard reached her and she frowned. She hurried to the window before she remembered this room faced the back of the house.

She dashed downstairs and yanked open the front door. An imposing man stood there and scowled at her. She stumbled back, grateful when Merlin pressed his body against her legs. "Mr. Gordon. I didn't expect to see you so soon."

His frown deepened as he looked around. "I can tell. Haven't you done any work in here yet?"

Enough was enough. She'd had it with this family and their holier-than-thou attitudes. "Maybe you would have been able to tell the difference if you had visited your sister more often or at least if you had come here after she passed."

Randolph Gordon pushed his way into the hall. "Ms. Stevens, when my daughter called me to notify me of your bad attitude, I couldn't believe it. But after your disrespectful display, I can believe she's right. I should have hired a more reputable company to clean my house."

"You mean *my* house," she shouted. "Your sister's ghost came to me and proclaimed me the rightful heir to her home. You and your awful daughter have no right to her home. Get out. This house wants me here, not you and definitely not Lydia. You didn't care about this place when you lived here, and you don't care now. When I find the Master Key, you'll have the final answer as to who this house belongs to."

"The key belongs to me. I told Henrietta so when she lived and she wouldn't give it to me."

Holly's hands balled into tight fists. "Did you ever wonder why? It's because she knew your heart. You would corrupt the house and all it contains. All the doorways that lead to wonderful places would be in danger if you had your way. I don't intend to stand by and let you ruin Henrietta's home."

Randolph's face turned purple and he shoved Holly to the floor. "How dare you, you insolent nobody. I'll destroy you and your precious reputation if you don't get out of here right now."

Her back hit the bottom step and she winced. Sharp pain in her wrist didn't register as anger built, and her hands shook. She'd always heard the phrase, seeing red, but now it was her turn to experience it. This pompous, overbearing man dared to come here and threaten her? All on the word of his awful daughter? He'd told her when he hired her, he respected her reputation and honesty. She wouldn't sit here, afraid of the Gordons and not defend herself. She pushed up and winced again at the pain in her wrist.

She saw Ray come up to the front door, followed by Lucas and his brother. She gestured for them to wait where they were. "Stay there, guys. I can handle this. I've defended myself against people like this for most of my life."

Her chest heaved as she tried to suppress the rage that rose inside her. "How dare you? If you kick me out, I'll sue you for breach of contract. You said I had thirty days and then you signed it. If you kick me out before the contracted time is up, I'll have the upper hand in this fight. It isn't just my reputation at stake here, Mr. Gordon, but yours as well. So why don't you haul yourself up to the B and B and we'll talk about this tomorrow, when you can be a little more reasonable. It will be the last day of my contract with you, and we can settle this to your satisfaction."

"Don't you dare threaten me, girl." He glared down at Merlin. "If your beast has any diseases and my daughter gets ill because of his attack, you'll hear from my lawyer."

"Your daughter started it when she kicked my cat. I've hit the point where I don't care about your threats." She scratched Merlin's head. "And I don't threaten, sir. I promise. Now, get out of my house."

As Randolph Gordon stomped down to his waiting limo, Holly sagged against the doorframe. Ray and the Callahans hurried over to her. "Are you all right?" Ray said.

"I'm fine, except my wrist hurts, but I'll live. What a pompous, arrogant jerk. I can't believe he tried to throw me out and then threatened to sue me."

Ray pointed up the street at his neighbors who came out to watch the confrontation. "Well, you gave the people here hope. We're glad you're here, Holly."

"Me, too." She waved at the people on the sidewalk. "Would you guys like to take a break? I picked up some lemonade the other day."

They all pushed against each other to get to the

kitchen first. Holly smiled. "I have enough for all of you. Sit down while I get the glasses."

While they all snacked on the cookies, Miss Dee showed up with the promised cinnamon rolls. "Randolph just stormed into the B and B. I don't think I've ever seen him in such a snit."

"I'm responsible for that particular snit," Holly said. "I think I'm the first person since Henrietta to tell him no and to leave this house."

Dee nodded. "Very brave of you to stand up to him. Have you found the Master Key yet?"

Holly shook her head. "No, but the keyring decided to fall on the floor again. The keys stopped doing it for a while, but now they started again. I'm sure it has a deeper meaning than I initially thought."

"I guess we'll know soon enough." Dee accepted a glass of lemonade and smiled as the guys all reached for the rolls at the same time. "How much more work do you boys have on the fence?"

"It's going to take another day at least," Lucas said. "If the B and B can spare Parker, I can spare Ray and they can continue on it until it's done."

"Of course I can." Dee turned to Holly. "How's the cleaning coming along?"

"Quicker than I expected. I should have the third floor done by tomorrow, which is a good thing because that's the last day of my contract." She gazed up. "I still have to get up in the attic. Henrietta said she keeps her Christmas decorations up there. However, since I don't plan to leave, I'm going to tackle the attic last."

Dee rose and picked up the basket, now empty of cinnamon rolls. "I'll let you folks get back to work. Call me if you need help or more cinnamon rolls. I'll keep an eye on the Gordons. I don't think they'll cause any more problems." She winked. "Well, not for you at least."

They waved to her as she left and the four of them went back to their tasks. As Holly worked on the third-floor rooms, Henrietta appeared to her. "I'm sorry I didn't come to you sooner. Randolph's voice brought back too many bad memories."

"I don't blame you. He scared me at first, but then he made me so mad." She rubbed the oak dresser with her beeswax mixture in silence. She winced when she forgot her wrist hurt. "I've got to find the Master Key."

"You're very close to it, Holly. I can't tell you where it is, but I can tell you, you're almost there. The autumnal equinox is tomorrow. I feel it will be the most important one we've ever had."

Holly turned and her response died in her throat. The ghost had faded away. "I'm glad I've gotten used to her contact." She smiled at Merlin, who sat in the middle of the floor, washing his face. "At least I don't black out anymore."

Chapter Twenty-Eight

She worked through lunch, and she checked her phone and saw it had turned over to seven o'clock. How had the time slipped away from her? She hurried downstairs and walked outside. The Callahans had left for the night and Ray sat on the porch.

He turned at her approach. "I waited for you to get done. Would you like to go get some dinner?"

"I'd love to. Let me clean up a little. Did you need to go home to freshen up?"

He smiled. "I already did. Go get ready. I want to sit here and enjoy the night air."

Holly was in and out of the shower in less than ten minutes, then dressed quicker than usual. She took a couple of pain relievers for the ache in her wrist. They held hands as they walked into the diner and she waved to Sally. The same man who had left when they were there before sat at the counter in the same seat. Ray stared at him and frowned.

"I don't think the seating at the counter is too good tonight," Ray said loud enough to make sure all the patrons could hear him. "Let's grab a booth instead."

When they sat and picked up their menus, they dissolved into quiet laughter. Sally brought their drinks over and winked at them.

"Did you see his face?" Holly said when she could breathe. "He looked like he would fall off the stool. I don't think I've ever heard this place go silent in all the times we've come here."

"I've wanted to tell him off for years." He took her hand in his. "You gave me the courage to do it. Dark Landers aren't supposed to be pushovers and I've proved I refuse to be one anymore."

"I don't think you were ever a pushover. You're too nice to be as rude as other people." She smiled at him and squeezed his hand. "But I'm glad I could help you find the strength you always had in you. This town is in for some big changes, and it will be because of you."

"And you," he said. "Most definitely you."

****

Holly couldn't sleep when she went to bed. Merlin curled up by her head and purred in her ear. The soft rumble quieted her sleep for a little while, but she began to toss and turn again. Henrietta said the autumnal equinox would be the most important one in a long time. Did she mean Holly would find the Master Key tomorrow? Would Randolph and Lydia come here and sabotage all her hard work? Would she be removed from what she considered to be her home by force?

She reached out in her sleep and quieted down when Merlin's soft fur filled her hand. He purred louder and laid his paw on her cheek. Dreams came at her fast and she tossed and turned again until Merlin crawled onto her chest.

She couldn't wait for the sun to rise and put an end to all the questions in her mind.

****

Holly yawned when the sun shone in her eyes, and she stumbled downstairs to get breakfast. Merlin yawned from the middle of the kitchen table. "You didn't sleep great either, huh, buddy. We're in fine shape to work on the third floor today."

She ate and washed her dishes, then headed upstairs to put on her work clothes. She gathered her supplies and started on the last two rooms. The atmosphere in the house felt calmer and warmer the more she brought it back to its former glory. As soon as Ray and the Callahan brothers got the yard in shape, the house would be perfect.

She'd almost finished another room when, once again, a furious pounding on the front door pulled her away from her job. She grumbled about unimportant interruptions as she stomped down to the first floor.

"All right, hang on a second," she shouted. She didn't need this nonsense so early in the morning. She flung open the front door, not surprised to see Randolph glaring at her with Lydia behind him, smiling her smarmy smile. "I don't have any more to say to you. Today is the deadline and I'll be finished before the sun goes down."

Randolph laughed in her face. "You can't have this house. I promised it to Lydia. She's the rightful heir."

Holly laughed at him. "I'm the rightful heir. Henrietta said so."

"You're a dreadful liar. You haven't talked to my sister's ghost, and you aren't the rightful heir. When you finish the job, I want you gone."

"Is there a problem here, Holly?" Ray said behind the Gordons.

"No, Ray. We don't have a problem, right, Mr. Gordon?"

Randolph pushed his way into the house and

marched over to the rolltop desk. He picked up the keyring and shook them in Holly's face. "Where is the Master Key? You've lied about a lot of issues, so I'm sure you've lied about not finding the key. Where is it?"

"I've never lied to you about anything that happened here. And I don't have the key," she shouted back. "If I did, I sure wouldn't give it to you."

Ray pushed by Randolph to stand by Holly's side. "She doesn't have it, Randolph. Go back to the B and B. We're almost done here, then you can come back and look for the key."

Dee and Adelaide walked inside, followed by Lucas and Parker. Behind them came the mayor and the town elders. "We all felt the need to be here now," Dee said. "The house's magic summoned us. We've all felt a pulse radiate out from here. Holly, what's happened?"

Holly glanced around the room. "Henrietta's here. She's upset Randolph has come inside. She told him never to return to her home and Lydia would never take her place."

"And now you lie again, Ms. Stevens?" Randolph said. "Pitiful."

Holly took Ray's hand. "All of you have been called here to bear witness to the rightful heir take her place as Keeper of the Keys," Holly said in a voice not her own. "The autumnal equinox has arrived and with it, the crowning of the new Keeper."

Merlin stretched up and jerked the keyring from Randolph's hand. He sauntered over to drop it at Holly's feet. She bent down and picked it up. A low hum started and began to grow in volume and strength. Holly took Ray's hand in her right, and the keyring in her left. Merlin placed a paw on her foot and Ray's.

"Behold, the Master Key beckons."

The keyring began to glow and rainbow light encompassed Ray, Holly, and Merlin. One by one, each key glowed with its own unique light. The ring floated up and all the keys pointed to the stairs. Holly almost floated as she headed toward the staircase. Ray, Merlin, and the crowd followed her as she walked upstairs.

The keys stopped in front of the white door on the third floor. The keys floated in front of the door and waited for Holly. She grabbed the keyring and took Ray's hand again. Merlin sat down and looked up at them. They laid their hands against the door and Merlin laid his paw on it also. Rainbow light shot out and flowed through the house. She turned the knob and the door opened.

She looked around Henrietta's bedroom for real this time. She felt Henrietta leave her and the ghost stood off to the side. She knew the key would be in here, but still didn't know where. She had finally accessed this room and one more condition needed to be fulfilled. The three of them, because Merlin refused to be left behind, walked into the room.

Holly and Ray each took a side of the keyring and held it. Merlin placed his paws on their feet once again. The rainbow light flowed back into the room and surrounded them. As it did, a large, brass key formed in the light. It twirled in a quick, tight circle, then slowed down to float in front of Holly. Ray smiled and nodded at her as Henrietta's ghost looked on.

She took a deep breath and reached out to grab it. The other keys heated up until she touched the Master Key to the ring. The keys settled down and each light surrounded its own key. Holly stood there, and the keys dangled from her hand. She gazed at the crowd who followed them and smiled.

"Let's head back downstairs where we can be more comfortable," Holly said.

The large group walked down to the living room, Merlin in the lead, Henrietta's ghost behind. Holly clutched the keys to her chest and held tight to Ray's hand. The Master Key had been found and Henrietta was right. She didn't need to ask any other questions. The key itself answered all the questions in her mind.

"The key is mine," Lydia yelled when they walked in the living room. She tried to snatch it from Holly and grabbed Holly's arm. The keys lit up and their light blasted her backward, and she tripped and fell. "Father, make them give me the key."

Randolph helped Lydia to her feet before he turned on Ray and Holly. "You heard her. Hand it over."

"It doesn't work like that, brother, and you know it," Holly said in Henrietta's voice again. "Holly is the rightful heir to my home. You and Lydia are banished from here. Don't ever come back. You aren't welcome here, now or ever." Holly looked at everyone in the living room. "You are all witnesses to this event. The new Keeper of the Keys has been chosen and it is Holly Stevens."

Miss Dee applauded, and the rest of the people followed suit. Randolph's face turned purple with rage. "You will hand over the key and leave this house."

Holly walked up to him. "Randolph, I believe you should return to wherever you call home. Be it New England or the Dark Lands. You belong in one of those places, but not here. Never here in Garland Falls again."

Randolph grabbed the key and the rainbow light brightened and surrounded his hands. A scream tore itself from his throat as a shockwave blasted out to throw everyone backward. Light filled the room, and circled Holly and Ray. Randolph slid across the floor on his side, and Lydia stumbled after him.

She helped her father to his feet and stared at his hands. Dark red blisters covered his palm where he had grabbed the Master Key. The house had made its choice, along with the ghost of its former owner. The Gordons wouldn't be welcome in the house or the town ever again.

Randolph looked at the mayor and the town elders to get their support, but they backed away a few steps. Lydia clung to her father's arm and took in the unfriendly looks from the small crowd. No one wanted to be near the Gordons, now that the house and Henrietta's ghost had chosen the heir to the keys.

Mayor Jacobs stepped up to Randolph. "I think you should leave Garland Falls now. Do us and yourself a favor, Randolph. Don't ever come back." As soon as the Gordons stomped toward the front door, the mayor turned to Ray. "I hope, in time, you'll forgive my attitude toward you. You must understand, old prejudices will fade slowly, but it will happen. Ms. Stevens, come by my office and I'll make sure all the paperwork for this house will be in order. You will be listed as the owner and sole inheritor to Henrietta Gordon's fortune."

"Thank you, mayor," she said. "I get a fortune?" She turned to Ray and grinned. "I'm glad we got engaged before I found out I was rich."

He pulled her to his side, before he turned his

attention to the mayor and the town elders. "I understand, mayor," Ray said. "But you need to understand this. I won't put up with insults from anyone any longer, no matter who says them."

"Understood." The mayor turned to the assembled people. "Since we have a new Keeper, I think we had all best get back to our own businesses. We have a celebration to attend and tourists to make happy. There will be a lot of paperwork to make sure all this is taken care of in the proper and legal way. We'll make the announcement tonight at the opening ceremony."

Holly and Ray followed everyone down to the first floor. They thanked Miss Dee, Mrs. Hall, the Callahans, and all the town elders. Soon, they were alone in the hall. Holly walked into the living room. She couldn't believe the house was hers, but not hers alone. She smiled at Ray, happy he would be a big part of her future.

She wrapped her arms around Ray's waist. "I think you should kiss me now."

"You always have the best ideas."

He gently touched his lips to hers and she melted against him. Who knew one kiss would be so wonderful. She still held the keys and they continued to vibrate in her hands. Would they ever stop or did they react in response to her emotions? As Ray held her, she didn't care. The keys could do whatever they wanted as long as she had Ray with her.

Chapter Twenty-Nine

After Ray left for the night, Holly walked up to Henrietta's bedroom. The Master Key opened the white door, and she knew the rest of the doors would open now. "Henrietta, are you here?"

The ghost faded into view. "I'm here. You handled yourself very well against my brother. I'm glad you've come home to Garland Falls."

"Thank you, but you were a big part of helping me stand up to him." Holly thought about what Henrietta had told her. "I've never been here before, so how could this be my home?"

Henrietta gestured to one of the chairs and waited until Holly sat. "Adelaide told you she thought you might be distantly related. I believe she's right. I sensed the powerful magic in you. You had to be here Garland Falls for your magic to get jump started, which is why I chose you. You're a very special woman, Holly Stevens. You even helped Ray find his voice and his courage to stand up for himself. I didn't like to see him be treated the way he'd been all these years."

"Thanks for your faith in me and Ray." She looked up at the ghost. "You know, I couldn't have done any of this without you. Henrietta, since I have the Master Key and the house, you won't leave, will you? I'd love for you to stay with us."

"Of course, I'll stay as long as you need me."

Henrietta smiled. "Do you think you'll be able to handle the door to the Dark Lands now? After all, the doorkeeper on the other side scared you the first time you two met. He's not such a bad sort once you get to know him."

"I've got his number now and he won't get to eat Merlin." She picked up her cat and scratched him behind his ears. "I suppose I'll need to move the cabinet I shoved in front of it."

Henrietta floated over to the large, canopy bed. "Holly, I want you to have my bedroom. There are other rooms where I can go when you and Ray get married, and you two can have some privacy."

"Are you sure? This is your room."

"Not anymore. You own the house and everything in it, and it includes this room." She reached out to stroke Holly's cheek and the cold made Holly shiver. "Take this room with my blessing."

Holly walked to the bed and ran her hand down the bedspread. Her cheeks heated at the thought of herself and Ray in this room. Well, those thoughts were for another day. She'd move her clothes and toiletries from the second-floor room up here tomorrow. Merlin jumped on the bed and stared at her. She stroked his back as she picked him up.

"And your fine gentleman there may have his own magic to share with you in the future," Henrietta said as she faded away.

"This is our home now, Merlin." She gazed around the room, so happy she had this wonderful house. "And I have magic and suspect you might, too. I mean, you showed up out of nowhere and we bonded the minute we looked at each other. Who knew?" Merlin stuck his tongue out at her and jumped down. "All right, all right. I guess you knew. You are one smart, magical cat."

****

The next day, Ray and Parker Callahan showed up to get back to work on the fence. Holly watched them from the front window and smiled. Soon, this house would look as it did in its heyday. Time to get back to work, so she started with moving the cabinet from in front of the purple door.

She gave it a hard shove and pushed it back to its original place. She walked back to the door and Merlin sat by her side. She looked down at him and gave him a thumbs up. She inserted the purple key, unlocked the door, and opened it. The land hadn't changed from the brief glimpse she'd gotten before.

The little man stared at her. "So, you found the Master Key. Welcome to your new job, Keeper. Do not come to this land unless you are invited. Until then, I wish you luck."

He slammed the door in her face and Holly bit back a smile. Joy bubbled up at the fact she no longer feared the man and the land he lived in. She took the keyring now with the Master Key and unlocked the yellow door in the hallway. The lock turned and it looked like what Ray described to her. A small room held the atmosphere of safety and security. She didn't have to check the other doors. She knew now she could go through them whenever she wanted, except the purple one. She would definitely wait for that invitation.

One key decorated with a tree began to glow with a golden light. She closed her eyes and let the key guide her to where she should go. In the library, a door on the back wall had the same golden light and the same carving. Holly inserted the key into the lock and opened the door. A tall, beautiful woman stepped through.

"I'm pleased to meet you, Holly Stevens," she said. "You will be a strong Keeper of the Keys."

"Thank you, but I'm not sure who you are."

"I'm Ray's mother." She took Holly's hands in hers and kissed her cheek. "He's told me much about you. You are as lovely as he said."

Holly's cheeks warmed at the compliment. "Thanks again. I like Ray very much and I'm happy to meet you."

Ray's mother squeezed her hands. "It's my turn to thank you. My son has never had such a wonderful person defend him. He's had to put up with so much negativity. I'll be forever grateful to you for being his friend and soon his partner for life."

"He's such a wonderful, kind man. I want everyone to see him as I do." She grinned. "They won't have a choice, if I have my way about it."

"You're a good person, Holly. You have a good soul. We'll talk again soon. Give Ray my love."

"I will."

Holly walked back to the front window to watch the man she had fallen in love with work on their home. She loved the fact they owned the house on Darkling Street. It became easier to call the house theirs every time she thought it. In the future, the house would be filled with love, laughter, and from her vision, a passel of children.

****

The house on Darkling Street would no longer be the house everyone feared. It would now be a place of welcome for anyone who needed it. Merlin meowed and curled up on the couch as Henrietta looked on. Yes, Holly and Ray were the right people for her former home. She and Merlin glanced at each other. Of course, she'd have to stick around for a while, to make sure there weren't any future problems.

After all, they loved their town of Garland Falls and anything could happen here. Even a spooky house could become a haven for those who needed it. Like Holly said at the start, it just needed some TLC, fresh air, light, and whole lot of love.

A word about the author…

I graduated from Mercy High in Baltimore, MD in 1981 and got married to an Air Force man in 1982. We have two amazing boys who have grown into amazing young men. We spent sixteen years in southern New Jersey, four of them at McGuire AFB and the rest near Atlantic City. Always a fan of fairy tales, myths, and folklore, I try to use those kinds of settings in my books. Visit my website at
www.annettemillerauthor.com

Thank you for purchasing
this publication of The Wild Rose Press, Inc.

For questions or more information
contact us at
info@thewildrosepress.com.

The Wild Rose Press, Inc.
www.thewildrosepress.com

9 781509 259045